Ecstasy Romance®

"YOU DON'T WANT TO GET MARRIED AGAIN, DO YOU?" SHE CRIED.

"Rachel, listen to me. I don't want us to make the same mistake twice, that's all."

"I see," she said stiffly.

"No, you don't," Rafe said harshly. "You want to do the same thing again, rush in without thinking, without trying to understand—"

"Oh, I understand. I understand that you're a man who lives for the moment, right? You like your freedom. You grab at life, Rafe. You're a taker. A selfish, grabbing hustler."

"You've got it wrong, Rachel. I love you; you've got to know that. It's just . . . I don't want to put either of us through that pain again." He grasped her shoulders. "Don't you see what I'm telling you?"

"What you're telling me," Rachel murmured coldly, "is that you're a coward."

CANDLELIGHT ECSTASY CLASSIC ROMANCES

CANDLELIGHT ECSTASY ROMANCES®

RESTLESS YEARNING

Alison Tyler

A CANDLELIGHT ECSTASY ROMANCE®

Published by
Dell Publishing Co., Inc.
1 Dag Hammarskjold Plaza
New York, New York 10017

ISBN: 0-440-17452-X

Printed in the United States of America

February 1987

10 9 8 7 6 5 4 3 2 1

WFH

To Our Readers:

We have been delighted with your enthusiastic response to Candlelight Ecstasy Romances®, and we thank you for the interest you have shown in this exciting series.

In the upcoming months we will continue to present the distinctive sensuous love stories you have come to expect only from Ecstasy. We look forward to bringing you many more books from your favorite authors and also the very finest work from new authors of contemporary romantic fiction.

As always, we are striving to present the unique, absorbing love stories that you enjoy most—books that are more than ordinary romance. Your suggestions and comments are always welcome. Please write to us at the address below.

Sincerely,

The Editors
Candlelight Romances
1 Dag Hammarskjold Plaza
New York, New York 10017

RESTLESS YEARNING

CHAPTER ONE

"I love weddings," Rachel Mason said effusively, greeting her sister, Norah, with a warm embrace.

"Especially when they're not your own," Norah said teasingly.

A tiny shadow crossed the features of Rachel's face. She was generally adept at keeping her feelings under wraps, but around her older sister, that guard sometimes faltered. Particularly now. Being back on Kincaid Island made Rachel feel especially vulnerable.

"I'm sorry," Norah said, apologizing quickly, and brushing a strand of chestnut-brown hair from her face, mindlessly tucking it behind her ear. "That was hitting below the belt. I guess it's nerves." She lifted a towel from the bench on the side of the private tennis court and dabbed at her slender neck.

Rachel took Norah's hand. "It's only natural to have a few butterflies in your stomach, Norah. But Josh Kincaid is a terrific man."

"I know what's going through that mind of yours. Not like his reckless, irresponsible, erratic, impossible younger brother, Rafe. There, did I get all of the right adjectives in?"

Rachel had to laugh. "I could think up a few more, if so inclined. Which I'm not, I hasten to add. I stopped thinking about my disastrous marriage five years ago." She looked up toward the sprawling stone mansion, the Kincaid family's summer retreat and second home. "Give or take a few months."

Norah followed Rachel's glance. "I guess being here on the island after all this time brings back memories," Norah said softly. "If you want to know the truth, I've been more nervous about how you would react to . . . being here than how I'm reacting." She crossed her arms. "I still find the island claustrophobic. I thought I would go crazy that summer I came up here to help you prepare for your wedding. I find tiny islands more than a bit confining."

"The Kincaids always have their weddings here on the island. It's tradition." There was a wistful tone in Rachel's voice. Her ten-month marriage to Rafe Kincaid might have been a disaster, but the wedding that summer she'd turned twenty-one had been pure perfection. She and Rafe had come to Kincaid Island off the Connecticut coast weeks before the actual ceremony; that had been part of the tradition too. It had been a time devoted to getting to know the Kincaid family, participating in the wedding plans, swimming, sailing, and lying on the beach getting a beautiful tan to set off her designer-original, formal, lace-and-satin wedding gown. Rachel had loved every minute of it.

"You were always a sucker for tradition, yourself." Norah sighed, tucking her tennis racket into its case.

"Listen, I'm glad you caught me out here, and it's been fun chatting, but we can do more of that later. Let's get you up to the house and unpacked and all that." She paused. "I was so pleased when you called this morning and said you could start your month's vacation a few days early. And you timed your arrival perfectly; we'll have a few uninterrupted hours before the hordes are due to descend." Norah felt Rachel tense. "Relax, I just meant Josh, his folks, and Liz Eastman, an interior decorator who's going to do some work on the house for the wedding. Oh, and Ned Welles, Josh's business partner. But he's arriving tomorrow morning. Then there will be no other guests until next week. And as for Rafe, I told you . . . he definitely isn't coming. I read you every word of that wire on the phone. He's off on assignment in Nicaragua. Another three weeks' minimum. So relax."

Norah swung an arm around Rachel. At five foot seven she was a good three inches taller than her younger sister. Norah had her father's build: slender, athletic, sturdy. And she had her father's warm brown eyes, his vibrant smile, and his free spirit. Rachel, on the other hand, was entirely her mother's child. Small, delicate, ethereally lovely with smoky slate-blue eyes, luxurious long hair the warm golden-brown color of cognac, and a lean, strong, beautifully proportioned body. And like her mother, Rachel Mason had an impetuous spirit . . . at least until her marriage to Rafe Kincaid had taught her that there was a stiff price to pay for impetuousness. She'd become far more serious-

11

minded and almost impossibly practical, according to Norah, since her divorce from Rafe.

"I am relaxed. It's just . . . well, you never know with Rafe. One day he's off photographing Contras in Nicaragua, the next day he's stretched out on a couch in Manhattan sipping a tequila sunrise."

"I see you still remember his favorite drink," Norah said, teasing her.

Rachel scowled. "I decided long ago it was better to keep a few things about Rafe Kincaid in mind, purely for my own protection. I don't believe in making the same mistake twice."

"Does that mean marriage in general or marriage to Rafe Kincaid in particular?" Norah queried as they followed the elm-covered gravel walk that took them past the horses' paddocks, the glistening sea-blue Olympic-size pool, and the glass-and-cedar gable-roofed cabana.

"I have absolutely nothing against marriage," Rachel said fervently, "to the right man. I just haven't met him yet, that's all."

"And what, pray tell, does Rachel Mason believe to be the right man?"

Rachel grinned. "You should know. You found him." There was no bitterness in Rachel's voice—only a touch of envy. Josh and Norah had met at Rachel and Rafe's wedding and had become instant friends. Over the years their friendship had grown into something more, and last Christmas they had announced that they were getting married. And despite the fact

12

that Josh was Rafe's brother, Rachel could not be happier for the couple; she also could not imagine a nicer man to have for a brother-in-law.

"Uh-oh. Do I have to be careful lest my little sister try to woo my fiancé out from under my nose?" Norah asked playfully.

"Would that I could," Rachel said, teasing her back. "But the man is obviously very attached to that Mason family nose of yours. The only nose, I might add that the man voted by Fortune as the most confirmed bachelor on Wall Street has ever been tempted by. Tell me, Sis, what is your secret?"

"I wish I knew. I might feel more like this whole marriage business made some sense. Here I am madly in love, and I still don't know what hit me. It's a bit unsettling. I may not have been Fortune's choice for the most confirmed bachelorette, but that's only because Fortune doesn't bother to report on poorly paid professors of French literature."

Rachel studied her sister. "You aren't sorry you turned down that offer at the Sorbonne in order to get married, are you?"

Norah shrugged. "A year in Paris at the leading French institution of learning? Then a second year traveling through France doing research on childrens' fairy tales? Of course I have a few misgivings," Norah admitted. "Unlike you, Rachel Mason, I have a bit of the wanderlust in me."

"That's because you were already off in college when Dad left Washington to be an ambassador of goodwill. You weren't carted off to parts unknown like Mom and I. First the Upper Volta and then Panama and last, but certainly not least, Senegal. Which reminds me, have you gotten word from the folks?"

"They promise to show up no later than the third. Which means they're likely to arrive on the fourth or fifth."

"As long as it's not the sixth," Rachel said, smiling. "Leave it to Dad to be caught up in some political squabble and miss his daughter's wedding. You'd think they'd be thrilled to get out of that torrid heat for a few weeks. I still can't believe they've remained there all these years. Dakar, Senegal would be the last place I'd choose to settle."

"As I recall, there was a time that you loved being in Dakar. I remember that summer I visited you all over there just before I started teaching at Columbia." Norah gave Rachel a sidelong glance. "In fact, speaking of wanderlust, hadn't you and Rafe just gotten back from a two-week excursion along the Gambia River? You were positively brimming with enthusiasm and excitement over the experience. Very exotic and rather dangerous, I thought at the time."

"You were right, it was dangerous. Our poor excuse for a cabin cruiser nearly capsized several times, a group of unfriendly natives almost fried us in oil for Sunday dinner, and it was a small wonder I didn't contract malaria. But Rafe had this photo assignment for *Time* magazine to do, and like a fool I let him talk me into joining him. Only the very young and the very

14

naive would have found that particular adventure, as well as a few others he convinced me to go along on, anything but harrowing."

Norah chuckled. "My, but haven't we become a stick-in-the-mud in our old age."

"I am not a stick-in-the-mud. Is there anything wrong with wanting to live a life that has some stability, security? I like being surrounded by familiar things. . . ."

"What of the old saying, 'Familiarity breeds contempt'?"

"Now you sound like Rafe."

"I sometimes wonder if Josh Kincaid hasn't opted for the wrong sister," Norah said reflectively. "Josh is as fanatic about roots as you are. And as strong on tradition and stability. No wonder he took over in the brokerage house when his father retired. Can you imagine Rafe exchanging his camera for an attaché case?"

Both sisters giggled. "Or those ragged work shirts and chinos for a three-piece suit?" Rachel added.

"Never," Norah confirmed, swinging open the screen door to the house.

Lois Gordon, the small, wiry, middle-aged housekeeper, came scurrying into the hall from the kitchen.

"Mrs. Kincaid . . . I mean, Miss Mason." Lois flushed. "How . . . nice to see you after all this time."

"Please, Lois, I still prefer Rachel to . . . Miss

Mason. How are you? You haven't changed a bit in five years."

"Oh, I'm just the same, thanks. But my, you've grown up some." She scanned Rachel's sophisticated soft gray sundress and the matching jacket draped over her arm.

Rachel laughed. "A bit of a change from the cutoffs and tank tops I ran around in that summer. Or rather, the bikinis I practically lived in when no one but you and Rafe were around—" Rachel stopped abruptly, aware that her cheeks had turned crimson. She'd mentioned Rafe's name so naturally. It had just rolled off her tongue without the usual split second of hesitation. Being back here on the island was indeed stirring memories. What was worse, they were happy memories.

Norah touched Rachel's shoulder lightly. "I'm going to run up and shower." She turned to Lois. "Could you ask Ted to pick up Rachel's things from the dock? Oh, and I'd adore a gin and tonic."

"What about you, Miss . . . Rachel?" Lois asked.

"A wine cooler would be fine. If I drink anything stronger, it will go straight to my head."

Norah was halfway up the sweeping flight of stairs. "More's the pity, Rachel Mason. It seems to me you could use a little something to loosen you up a bit."

Rachel was about to retort when the phone rang.

"I'll get it," Norah said, racing back down the stairs. "It's probably Josh."

Rachel wandered into the large, airy living room.

16

She had always loved this room; it reminded her of something out of an Italian villa with its cool terracotta floors, plaster walls with a mottled matte surface that looked like a gently aged fresco, and three arched French windows facing out on a courtyard replete with a stone fountain. The furniture was a combination of formal and rustic: Queen Anne tables, a creamy white modern sofa, a wicker rocker, and a Louis XIV chaise lounge.

Despite the heat outside, the elegant room was cool. Large, colorful vases filled with lilies of the valley, and wild roses gave off a delicate scent that mingled with the fresh sea air. Rachel walked over to the dramatic stone fireplace, running her slender fingers across the rough granite. She slipped off her sandals, her feet sinking luxuriously into the thick white lambswool area rug in front of the hearth. How many times had she and Rafe lain here in front of a roaring fire locked in each other's arms in a mad, passionate embrace?

Her mind drifted back to one afternoon in particular, after a storm. They'd been out horseback riding when they were caught in a torrential summer downpour. They'd been fighting too. Rachel had wanted to spend the whole summer honeymooning on the island, before settling in Rafe's brownstone residence in Manhattan, but Rafe had just received a call that morning, offering him an assignment in Cape Verde. He thought it a perfect idea to extend their honeymoon by combining it with a little business.

"I thought you were going to stick to assignments in

the States," Rachel had said petulantly as they'd raced into the house, drenched to the bone.

"I thought you'd like the idea of Cape Verde. It's close to Senegal. We could stop off and visit your folks."

"I just saw my folks three weeks ago at our wedding, remember?"

"We wouldn't be leaving until the end of August. And we won't have to stay for more than three weeks. Will you at least think about it?"

Rachel was pulling off her sodden riding boots and socks. "I knew you had no intention of keeping your word," she mumbled. "Promises. They mean about as much to you as . . . as our wedding vows, I suppose."

A hand trailed down her wet T-shirt. "Our wedding vows mean a lot to me, Rachel. As for the rest, I never actually promised I'd never take another foreign assignment. I'm a photojournalist, after all. And the best jobs are overseas." He slowly lifted her shirt up as he spoke, his fingers caressing her moist skin.

Rachel suppressed a shiver, her eyes meeting Rafe's. His angular, masculine, deeply tanned face was shiny from the rain, his incredibly thick lashes darker now that they were wet. And those relentless blue eyes were sparkling. He smiled. Years of rugged outdoor living had deepened the lines at the corners of his mouth and in the creases near his eyes. They became especially prominent when he smiled. He raked his fingers through his wet, carelessly long dark hair, pushing some wayward strands off his face.

Rafe Kincaid was not so much handsome as compelling. Three months ago he had swept Rachel off her feet. She'd found him irresistible, as he had her. It was the most passionate, inflamed courtship either of them could ever imagine. As Rafe lifted the wet T-shirt over her lacy white bra, his piercing blue eyes raking over her face, Rachel knew that he was as irresistible as ever.

Slowly, methodically, he began stripping her completely naked in the hallway. Rachel remembered being grateful it was Lois's day off and that the rest of the Kincaids had returned to their home in Connecticut; she was not sure that Rafe Kincaid could be trusted to act with the slightest degree of decorum when his desires were aroused. As he lifted her in his arms and carried her into the living room, gently lowering her to that thick, white lambswool rug, Rachel, too, was beyond caring about anything but the blinding passion Rafe inspired. He'd made a roaring fire in the hearth, then stood in front of it, undressing. Again his movements were languorous, utterly unselfconscious. He had a magnificent body, bronzed to perfection, sinewy with hard muscle, his torso lean with long legs. He was strong, muscular, a supremely physical man with an air of danger and excitement that exuded from every pore of his body. Rachel remembered the first time she'd laid eyes on him: She'd thought him the most provocatively sensual man she'd ever seen.

He dropped down to the rug, the heady scent of his cologne making her nose and the back of her throat tingle. Rachel could feel the warmth of his breath against her ear as he teasingly bit her lobe. She shivered with desire. . . .

"Rachel? Oh, there you are," Norah said. "Are you okay?" she asked, concerned by the stark look of surprise in her sister's expression.

"What? Oh . . . yes. I'm . . . fine." Rachel stammered, wrenched from her reverie. She was not only unsettled by the unbidden fantasy but also by the sheer intensity of the feelings that her fantasy had elicited. Her body had responded with startling arousal, the vision of Rafe disturbingly real.

Norah wasn't convinced that Rachel was all right, but she wasn't about to press the issue now. "Listen, that was Josh's mom. I'm sorry, but I'm going to have to leave you stranded here; I have to meet her and Josh in Greenwich. She is in an absolute tizzy over something to do with the caterers. She got Josh to promise we'd both go over there and try to help her straighten things out."

"Go ahead, don't worry about me; I'll be fine," Rachel assured her, some of the color returning to her face now.

"The thing is, I have a dress fitting tomorrow evening, so it makes the most sense for me to stay and come back to the island on Wednesday. And the Kincaids have decided to stay in town until at least then. I'm not sure about Liz—you know, the woman who's doing the decorating. She might wait until everyone else comes out."

"Norah, it's okay. I've spent time alone on this island before. Besides, Lois is here. To be honest, I wouldn't mind a couple of days to just unwind, take it easy. I'm beat."

"You work too hard, Rachel. I never thought you'd be the driven type."

"There's no leisurely way to be an associate producer of one of the top TV game shows in the country. *Sheer Madness,* is an appropriate name for it," she quipped.

"I still can't figure out how, of all the career choices you had, you opted for 'sheer' insanity."

"Actually, it's a lot of fun. One big happy, zany family. Besides, when I started on that show, I was feeling a little crazy myself. Rafe was gone so much of the time; our marriage was coming unglued fast. So the show was a match made in heaven." Rachel's eyes drifted down to the white lambswool rug. "Unlike my relationship with Rafe," she said in a barely audible voice.

Norah shook her head sadly. "You're still a little bit in love with Rafe, aren't you?"

Rachel smiled wistfully. "I suppose some part of me can't dismiss those few romantic months we spent together before everything fell apart, before I began realizing our getting married had been a terrible mistake, a crazy impulse." she admitted. "But believe me, I have no intention of allowing adolescent fantasies to interfere with reality. Absolutely no intention whatsoever," she said fiercely.

Norah studied her sister thoughtfully. "There's one thing I should mention, by the way. Josh's partner, Ned Welles, is still planning to arrive tomorrow morning. This is kind of his home away from home during the summer, and he's taken the next few days off. Another hard worker. He needs some unwinding time too. I think you'll like him. He's young, ambitious, popular. Oh, and very stable."

"Sounds promising," Rachel said brightly, but she wasn't fooling Norah.

"Rachel, what am I going to do with you? You give me these great speeches about wanting to find the right man, but every time a potential candidate comes along, you run the other way as fast as those gorgeous legs of yours can take you."

"That isn't true. It's just that I don't need a man, that's all. I'm a modern, independent woman," she said with a weak smile.

"And lonely as hell. You may be able to kid yourself, Sis, but whatever the time and age, love is one emotion that never goes out of style. Just look at me, for heaven's sake. I could have taken the prize for being the most modern, independent woman of all. And here I am racing off to quell a riot over whether the pheasants will or won't be served under glass for the reception dinner. And you want to know something, Rachel? When I'm not terrified out of my mind that I'm making the biggest mistake of my life, I feel

22

like I'm walking on cloud nine. Let's face it, I'm not a great beauty and I'm certainly never going to be up for a Pulitzer Prize. And yet quiet, serious, sometimes stuffy Josh Kincaid can make me feel like the most beautiful, clever woman that ever walked the face of this earth. Do you have any idea what that feels like?"

Lowering her gaze, Rachel murmured, "Yes. I know exactly how that feels."

Norah came over and put her arms around Rachel. "Sorry. I'm putting my foot in my mouth a lot today. Just as well I'm running off to Greenwich." She gave her sister a peck on the cheek. "You will be pleasant to Ned? He's really a nice man."

Rachel smiled. "I'll be positively charming. Okay?"

"Shall I ask Lois to stay over tomorrow night?"

"If this Welles character is as nice as you say, I'll assume I can trust him to behave like a proper gentleman. Of course, whether I behave as a proper lady depends on my own personal analysis of Ned Welles."

"You talk a good game, Rachel Mason, but that's all it is."

Rachel threw up her arms and grinned. "Please, Norah, give it a rest."

"Okay, okay. I'm going."

Lois arrived as Norah exited. "Shall I bring your wine cooler in here?"

Rachel quickly said no. She wanted a little distance from this room that had evoked such vividly erotic memories. "I'll have it on the patio. Afterward I'll change and go for a swim. Why don't you take off early, Lois? And if Ted's brought up my bags, there's really no reason for him to hang around this afternoon, either."

"What about your dinner?"

"I'll dig up something. Don't worry."

"Well, why don't I set out a cold plate for you?"

"That would be great."

It wasn't until close to ten P.M. that Rachel got around to eating the lovely salad topped with slivers of chicken and roast beef that Lois had prepared for her. She'd spent the afternoon and evening swimming, hiking, boating, and in general exhausting herself. Despite telling Norah that she was beat, Rachel felt a desperate need to keep herself physically occupied to ward off further thoughts and fantasies about Rafe Kincaid.

She'd eaten her dinner out on the patio, trying to ignore the romantic full moon overhead. Pushing the half eaten food away, she yawned, stretching her slender arms skyward. Then she cast a wary glance back at the house.

So many memories, she mused. She hadn't realized it would be this hard to return here after all these years. Upstairs on the third floor was the bedroom suite that she and Rafe had made their own that summer six years ago. It wasn't nearly as grand as the master suite on the second floor, but Rachel had loved the cozy feeling of the sloped ceilings, the old-fashioned flowery wallpaper, and the exposed beams, as well as the sensation of being on top of the world. The setting fit in perfectly with the feeling she had at the time that she, like Norah now, was floating on cloud nine. If only she'd known how awful the crash would be when that cloud had disappeared from under her.

She went into the house, realizing that she'd never inquired in just which room the handyman, Ted Lockwood, had put her bags. She paused in the hallway at the bottom of the stairs. The most likely place to find her luggage, she knew, was in the private suite on the third floor. She had hoped to avoid that area altogether on her stay here, but she climbed the stairs resolutely.

"The time has come, Rachel Mason," she said out loud, "to bury the memories once and for all."

Her luggage had not only been brought up to her old quarters, but also they'd been unpacked and put away. Before she could have second thoughts, Rachel quickly showered, slipped on a fire-red silk teddy, and crawled into the large brass bed. Despite her rapid heartbeat and her constant struggle to keep thoughts of Rafe at bay, it felt oddly comforting to be back in the familiar old bed. Surprisingly she fell asleep quickly, her body naturally, instinctively, moving over to the right-hand side of the bed. Rafe had always slept on the left.

She vaguely remembered waking sometime in the night to a dull, thudding noise, but then she drifted off again almost immediately. She figured Norah must have decided to come back to the island tonight, after all.

The second time Rachel woke, it was with a loud,

bloodcurdling scream as she felt the bed sag and a heavy weight fall across her hips. It took a split second to realize that the weight was a strong, very masculine arm.

"What the hell . . . ?" a man was muttering as she shrieked again.

In the midst of her hysteria Rachel heard the lamp on the bedside table crash to the floor. Then a large hand was reaching out, grabbing a hank of her hair, another hand trying to clamp down on her mouth as they struggled in the pitch dark.

Fear and shock mixed with outrage, especially as she realized that the man assaulting her was as naked as a bluejay. She managed to land a resounding smack against his face as she gasped for breath, struggling to keep that large hand from suffocating her. *This can't be happening to me,* she thought wildly. She clawed at his arm, finally getting his hand off her mouth. She let out another shriek, even though she knew there was absolutely no one besides this mad attacker and herself on the desolate island.

"Stop screaming, for chrissakes," a deep, raspy voice snapped.

Like magic, Rachel's next scream died instantly in her throat. Instead she emitted a long, astonished gasp. There was something stunningly familiar about that particular voice.

"That's better," he muttered, struggling to grab for the fallen lamp. "If you'd only let me turn this thing on to begin with . . ."

Suddenly the room was flooded with light.

"Rachel?" Rafe Kincaid sat bolt upright in bed and stared dumbfounded at his ex-wife.

Rachel's eyes drifted down the lean, muscular body that was as familiar as the voice. Then her eyes met his stunned gaze. "You never could be counted on to keep your promises, Rafe Kincaid. Why aren't you in Nicaragua?"

Rafe was still absorbing the shock and, for one of the rare occasions in his life, was speechless.

Whether it was pure relief at discovering that she was not about to be molested, after all, or whether it was seeing her cool, supremely confident ex-husband looking like he'd just swallowed a fly, Rachel suddenly burst into a fit of laughter.

CHAPTER TWO

"I don't find this particularly amusing, Rachel," Rafe said indignantly, yanking the thin cotton blanket off her in order to drape it around his naked body.

As Rafe's eyes took in her skimpy red teddy, Rachel's laughter came to an abrupt halt. She made a grab for the cover.

"What's the matter," he said, taunting, "not so funny when the shoe's on the other foot?" He caught her arm. "And talk about what I'm doing here, what are you doing here? When I phoned Josh from Kennedy Airport, he said you weren't due out until Wednesday or Thursday."

Rachel wasn't about to offer the information that she had spoken to Norah about her last-minute change of plans only that morning, and that her sister and Josh had probably crossed paths somehow. "And according to your wire, you weren't due out at all," she mumbled, getting out of the bed and stomping across the room to the closet, fully aware of Rafe's penetrating observation of her every step. Throwing on a robe, she whirled around to face him. He was now reclining languorously across the bed. All he needed was the tequila sunrise to make the picture complete.

"You look terrific, Rachel. The five years have been good to you. You've matured in all the right places." He'd clearly regained all of his cool confidence. It never did take Rafe very long.

"You still didn't answer me," she retorted. "What are you doing here?"

"What about me? How do I look?" he asked with a teasing grin, ignoring her question. "I mean, now that you've gotten such a thorough look."

"One thing about you hasn't changed," Rachel said with a chilly smile. "Your ego is still as big as ever. Now, if you don't mind, I'd like to get back to sleep."

"I don't mind at all." He grinned, moving over to the left side of the bed.

"Very amusing, Rafe. But I'm afraid you'll have to find yourself another room for the night."

"Five years is a long time, Rachel. Do you know, I haven't spent so much as a day on the island since we were here together six summers ago? And yet here we are, both ending up in the same room even though there are a dozen guest rooms in the house. I almost didn't, you know. Pick this room, I mean. Then I said to myself that it was crazy to avoid a room that held . . . so many exciting memories."

Rafe's intimate tone and his steady, seering gaze threw her completely off-balance. Her heartbeat quickened again. No longer afraid of being attacked by an unknown assailant, Rachel's pulse was now racing instead in fear of being seduced by a cunningly handsome ex-husband.

"We could rekindle a few memories," Rafe said in the deep, sexy voice that used to drive her crazy. "For old times' sake."

His blatant come-on was really what saved her from temptation. "And that's another thing that hasn't changed about you, Rafe Kincaid," she said with a defiant flick of her head. "You lack subtlety."

Rafe laughed. "You're right. I never did believe in beating around the bush." He sobered then. "If I recall, neither of us was too subtle in the old days. If we'd both played it a little closer to the chest, we probably never would have tied the knot."

"Fortunately we both came to our senses before too long. And just for the record, Rafe, I've learned how to be more subtle these days."

A dark brow arched with amusement. "I could take that remark as a challenge."

Rachel glared at him. "Don't waste your time."

He grinned. "I didn't say that I would." He stretched over the bed and snatched up his trousers from the floor, reaching into a pocket for a pack of Players cigarettes and a silver lighter. Another item that hadn't changed. He still smoked.

Rachel knew that he deliberately allowed the blanket to drift down around his hips, so that she could not avoid noticing once again his leanly muscled physique. His startling blue eyes rested on her as he lit a cigarette and sank back against the pillows. He held out the lighter toward her, a slim, rich, embossed silver design. "Remember?"

Remember? How could she forget? She'd bought him the lighter when they were first married. *To Rafe. Always. Rachel.*

"I thought you might have given up smoking by now," she said sullenly, hating him for awakening even more memories.

"Some habits are hard to break," he said, taking in a deep drag.

She stood clutching her robe around her slender frame, staring at him, knowing too well just how true those words were. She still found Rafe Kincaid as alluring and handsome as always—and as glib, taunting, and seductive. At twenty she'd found those qualities mesmerizing. But then, at twenty she was very naive. Besides, in those days, Rafe's disreputable charms were tempered by tenderness and a hint of vulnerability that made Rachel dare to think the two of them stood a chance together.

Neither of those subtler, more gentle qualities were in the least bit visible now. There was a cutting edge to Rafe's manner, a cool, biting quality that wasn't there before. The tenderness was gone. So, Rachel saw, was the vulnerability.

Her own feelings of vulnerability were another thing altogether. "Are you going to get out of that bed?" She cursed herself for the tremulous tone of her voice.

"Are you going to join me in it?" he asked nonchalantly.

"I happen to have been here first," she said haughtily.

"And I happen to own it," he pointed out with a casual sweep of his hand.

Rachel's lips compressed. "Very well . . ."

"Hold on," he relented. "I'll find another room." He threw the covers off. Rachel turned around to avoid any further temptation.

Rafe laughed. "You never used to be so modest."

She refused to turn back until she heard him zip up his pants. "I wasn't your ex-wife in my less modest days."

"True." His eyes lingered on her. There was a heavy silence. "Rachel?"

An involuntary shiver shot down her spine at the way his lips had formed her name, slowly, tantalizingly, a touch breathlessly. She was unaware of the fact that her own lips had parted.

But Rafe noticed. The sight was disturbingly tempting. He scowled. Rachel had walked out of his life once. And Rafe Kincaid was as fanatic as Rachel about never making the same mistake twice. He saw that she was waiting for him to say something more. The truth was, he wasn't at all sure what he'd meant to say. Seeing her was more unsettling than he cared to admit.

He grabbed his blue work shirt, a pair of worn leather sandals, and his duffel bag from the floor, then started across the room.

As his hand turned the doorknob he shot her a

glance over his shoulder. "Do you still have that funny little snore when you sleep?"

Rachel gave him a seering look as he walked out without bothering to shut the door behind him. She strode over and slammed it closed. Then she pivoted sharply on her heel and marched back to bed.

The lingering scent of Rafe's tangy cologne seemed to cling to the sheets. Rachel felt a shudder of old, familiar longing clutch at her. She shut her eyes tightly. Hot tears burned against the lids as she angrily denied that she was still completely under the spell of Rafe Kincaid. "Damn," she muttered, clutching the blanket.

For several hours she lay awake, lecturing herself about the folly of her feelings and reminding herself in arduous detail of all the reasons her marriage with Rafe had broken up. He was self-involved, absolutely unwilling to compromise, and he always put his own needs and desires first. The entire time they were together, he consistently got his own way, manipulating her with seduction, teasing banter, and promises.

Promises. Rafe had sworn he wouldn't take that assignment in El Salvador. They'd argued about it a dozen times, even before any actual job had been offered him. Rachel knew Rafe well enough to know he was positively itching to go. Never mind the newspaper headlines filled with gruesome tales of violence, never mind about the two English reporters who had been killed or the American TV cameraman who nearly had been beaten to death by a marauding band

33

of terrorists. Rafe never let a little thing like danger stand in the way of getting the kind of pictures that made him one of the most sought after free-lance photojournalists in the country.

She'd waited until Rafe sent her the wire from El Salvador saying that he'd be leaving that day for home. Some inexplicable force had kept her from acting on her decision until she was certain that he was all right. Once she knew he was returning, she resolutely packed her bags and left the town house off Central Park West that she and Rafe had called home for close to a year.

The memory of Rafe storming into her office at NBC studios the next day when he arrived from El Salvador was one that would remain indelibly printed on her mind, as well as on the minds of all of the staff of *Sheer Madness* who happened to be around the twenty-seventh floor that day.

Rachel's office was in actuality a small, partitioned section, one of three or four dozen covering the floor. It was a space that offered only meager visual privacy and absolutely no sound privacy at all.

That afternoon she was just finishing up her weekly production schedule when Rafe burst her door open and strode into her office. Besides the look of pure fury on Rafe's face, the other thing Rachel noticed immediately was the abrupt silence that accompanied his whirlwind entrance. Gone were the noisy conversations from the adjoining partitions. Even the clacking of typewriters had ceased.

"What the hell do you mean by that little disappearing act you pulled, Rachel?" His shout echoed off the walls.

Rachel was mortified. "We can discuss the matter after work," she said evenly.

"We can discuss the matter right now," he snapped, slamming the door closed, a rather futile attempt at privacy, since the walls of her office went up only six feet, leaving a gaping space of at least two more feet for their voices to carry quite effectively.

"Rafe, please. Obviously you're upset—"

"Upset? You think I'm upset?" He stalked her like a demented prowler. "Oh, I'm not upset, Rachel. You think just because I come home and find every stitch of my wife's belongings gone from our home—and along with them my wife, herself—that I'm upset?" He grabbed her shoulders and leaned ominously over her. For the first time in her life Rachel felt afraid of Rafe. She'd never seen him so livid, so close to losing control.

"Stop this," she whispered, her hushed tones no longer having anything to do with the fact that a good thirty people were tuned into every word.

"Not even a goddamn note." His fingers were digging painfully into her skin.

"You're hurting me, Rafe."

He let go of her, as if she had burned him. "Do you suppose that makes us even, Rachel?"

"I told you I was going to leave you if you took that assignment." She stared at him defiantly as he glared

35

at her. Struggling for courage, she said, "You knew from the start what kind of a life I wanted—that I needed to have a sense of permanence. I thought that once we were married, once we started thinking of having a family, you'd realize one or both of us couldn't constantly go traipsing around the globe, spending a few months in South America, another few months in the Middle East, and who knows where else. I grew up that way, Rafe. And I wasn't happy." Her speech concluded, she rested her head in her hands. "I couldn't go on like this. I just couldn't."

He grabbed her wrist, so that her head nearly hit the edge of the desk. "And so your solution is simply to pack up and leave? That's it? *Finito?*"

"Why torture ourselves if we know it can't work?" She made the question sound so reasonable, but inside she felt as though her whole world were coming apart. Was she doing the right thing? Was this really what she wanted—to sever the ties so quickly? She was so much in love with him. Suddenly, at that moment, the feeling flooded her. She opened her mouth to take it all back.

But Rafe cut her off before she'd gotten the first word out. "All right, Rachel. If that's the way you want it. We got into this whole . . . mess . . . impulsively. Why not end it the same way? I never did believe in belaboring a point." He walked to the door. "You can file for the divorce if you like. Call it incompatability, mental cruelty, emotional deficiency. In fact, why don't you just call it hell?"

"Call it hell." Those had been Rafe's last words to her. The divorce went through quickly, without contest. Rafe had been represented by his lawyer; he was off on an assignment in Paris at the time. It was a trip that Rachel had originally planned to join him on. Rafe had convinced her that they needed to get away, even though she was up to her neck in work. But he wove the old magic, painting an exquisite picture of romantic days and nights in the City of Lights. Not that Rachel didn't know that she'd end up spending most of those romantic days and nights alone while Rafe got caught up in his assignment. Still, she'd wanted to believe him. And things were tense between them. Maybe a few weeks in Paris would help. So with a lot of wrangling, reorganizing, and overtime, she managed to get three weeks off from the show.

And then, instead of going off to Paris, she was settling her divorce in Mexico. It was just as well that she'd gotten the time off, though. After the divorce Rachel felt horribly depressed. She stayed over in the little resort in Oaxaca and proceeded to cry her eyes out for a good part of the first two weeks. Everything had happened so fast. But then, that was so like Rafe. Once he made up his mind about anything, he always acted on it instantly. Rafe was driven by immediacy and by passionate determination.

Rachel drew the blanket up over her shoulders as the cool morning air drifted into her bedroom. She shivered, her gaze drifting over to the huge bank of windows that looked out on a million-dollar view of the bay. She rolled over in bed. Going over those rough times saddened and exhausted her. She finally fell off to sleep a little after seven A.M.

At first she thought it was only the patter of rain on the roof that had awakened her. But almost immediately she was aware of another presence in the room. She opened her eyes, not surprised to see that Rafe had returned, certainly irate.

"Are you going to make it a habit of popping into my room?" she asked indignantly, propping her head up.

"I brought you some freshly squeezed orange juice," he said casually, looking depressingly fit and hardy to Rachel's bleary, bloodshot eyes.

"Go away." In one continuous motion she pulled the cover up over her head and fell back onto the pillows.

"You always loved fresh orange juice brought to you in bed. Don't tell me you no longer—"

"I told you to leave me alone."

"Lousy day today. It's raining. Looks like it's not going to clear up."

She could hear him moving around the room. "I don't need a weather report, thanks," she muttered.

"I thought we could do a little catching up. Josh tells me you've made it to associate producer of that game show. I caught it a few times when I was in town." He paused. "Tell me something. What is it that possesses perfectly sane people to dress up like buffoons and allow themselves to be made perfect fools of

38

on your show? It can't be greed; the most anyone ever won when I saw the show was a crummy stereo and a year's supply of lawn fertilizer. There they were, bobbing for pickles, balancing dollops of whipped cream and a cherry on their noses while trying to break-dance, and all to be the one to beat the clock and become the proud owner of a pile of . . . manure. I just can't figure it."

Rachel's body grew rigid with outrage as Rafe went on lambasting her show. She forgot about returning to sleep and threw the covers off her head. "Have you finished your erudite analysis, Mr. Kincaid?"

"Well, I wouldn't say it was erudite. But accurate," he offered with a teasing smile.

"It just may interest you to know that *Sheer Madness* happens to be the number-one game show on television today," she said curtly. "And I happen to be thrilled to be part of their success. In fact, all modesty aside for the moment," she added airily, "I happen to bear credit for some of that success myself."

Rafe watched her little exposition with amusement. "Last night I said that you were all grown-up, Rachel. But I walk in here with a perfectly friendly peace offering and you go ducking under the covers, flying off the handle, pouting those pretty lips. I see, after all, that there's still a bit of the child left in you." He saw her scowl. "A very appealing bit, if you must know. I always was a sucker for that feisty little-girl quality. There were times it drove me . . . crazy."

Rachel's mouth clamped shut. She saw that in her

39

outburst the cover had fallen down around her waist. Rafe's eyes were watching the rise and fall of her barely concealed breasts as she breathed. She watched him move closer to the bed. He set the glass of orange juice on the side table, never shifting his gaze from her. She saw the glitter in his blue eyes, the aggressive angle of his jaw. She knew darn well what he had in mind. The problem was, it was in her mind too.

As he sat on the side of the bed his hand reached out, tentatively stroking her tousled hair. "Rachel . . ."

Her eyes rested on his mouth. She couldn't look anywhere else. Her pulse beat erratically. She could feel his fingers sliding lightly down her hair, shifting the strands as he cupped the back of her neck.

"No, Rafe," she murmured. But neither one of them took her protest to heart as his face came toward her. She felt the moist heat of his mouth closing on her lips, the insinuating movement of his tongue against her teeth. Her lips parted.

He wasn't playing fair. But Rafe didn't believe in playing fair. He took what he wanted. And as though those five years of firm resolve had been nothing more than a figment of her imagination, Rachel gave in to a desire that had flared the moment she'd set eyes on Rafe again. She let him lean her back onto the pillows, his tongue plundering the warm, moist recesses of her mouth, his kiss greedy with conquest.

It ceased to matter that she had ended their marriage years ago, that Rafe had not changed one iota in all that time. Rafe's caressing hands moved over the silky material of her teddy, his fingers spreading across her firm buttocks, arching her against him as he stretched out beside her.

She felt his warm breath against her throat as his lips pressed to the throbbing pulse beat. "Oh, Rachel. It's been so long." One hand slipped between her thighs.

Rachel moaned. "Rafe . . ."

"I knew this was what you wanted, Rachel. You shouldn't have wasted last night," he murmured as his mouth slipped down to the lace trim of the red teddy.

Rachel stiffened. There it was again, that cutting tone in his voice—a tone that seemed to revel in victory. He'd meant to seduce her all along. Revenge? The word pounded in her brain.

Suddenly she pressed her hands against his chest and gave him a fierce shove. Unprepared, Rafe found himself falling off the bed. "Are you crazy, Rachel?" he gasped, stunned by her drastic switch in behavior. "What's the matter?"

"You're still in top form, Rafe. Only you're wrong about that little girl in me. I'm grown up enough to be able to see right through you."

"Really?" He glowered, getting to his feet. "And what the hell is it you think you see?"

"I see a vain, egotistical man who can't stand the thought that he didn't get the last . . . laugh."

"Is that what you really think this was about? Having a good laugh?" He leaned over and seized her shoulders, half lifting her off the bed. "I suppose that means that you had a great chuckle at my expense when I went storming out of your office five years ago —you and all your *Sheer Madness* pals." He released her as he finished talking.

Rachel fell against the pillows but then immediately sprang up on her knees. "You loved making that grand exit. You loved humiliating me in front of the entire staff. Oh, it wasn't me who got the last laugh, Rafe Kincaid," she said, jabbing his chest with her index finger. "It was you." She grabbed at the blanket and held it up against her chest despite the fact that it was a little too late for modesty.

Rafe's gaze narrowed on her. For a moment there was a deathly silence. Rachel met his eyes levelly. Her anger shifted into a new tension that rippled through her. She saw that her palm had replaced her finger on his chest. His heartbeat was rapid. She abruptly dropped her hand down.

"You're right, Rachel." His tone was low. "I did have a good laugh. At myself. Not you. I was twenty-eight years old when we met. You might have been little more than a child, but I should have known better than to think I could turn a spoiled adolescent into a . . . real woman."

Rachel bristled. "I seem to recall plenty of times when you wondered if I was more woman than you could handle."

He leaned closer to her, an insinuating smile on his face. "That's true. But only in bed, Rachel. I won't

42

deny that you were a voracious little she-devil in the sack. I should have kept you in it more of the time."

"Why, you bastard . . ." Incensed, she grabbed the glass of orange juice, meaning to toss it in his face.

Rafe caught her arm just as she took hold of it. "Oh, so you want to play some more childish games, do you?"

They struggled for possession of the glass, Rafe pulling Rachel off the bed and onto the floor in the process. She grabbed the front of his shirt, half the buttons popping. The juice ended up all over both of them. Rachel pounded his chest. "Look what you've done to me," she shrieked, orange juice trickling down her hair onto her face.

The rest of the juice had landed in Rafe's lap. "You little fool. Why the hell don't you grow up . . ."

They both continued shouting at each other, which was why they didn't hear the knock on the door.

"Excuse me," a deep baritone said, his voice overly loud so he could be heard over Rafe and Rachel's screaming match.

They looked up, startled to see a man standing at the open door. Neither of them recognized the intruder, a tall, light-haired man in his early thirties, very attractive in an Ivy League way, wearing well-pressed chinos and a crisp, cool, white polo jersey. The stranger's mouth quirked in a smile as he focused his attention on Rachel. "Are you all right?"

Rachel glared at Rafe as she tried to pull the blanket back around her. But Rafe was sitting on it, and he

43

wasn't in the mood to be helpful. Rachel's face reddened as she looked up at the stranger, who made no attempt to avert his gaze.

"I'm sorry, I didn't mean to intrude, but I was concerned." He paused. "I should introduce myself. I'm Ned Welles. Josh invited me. I work—"

"I know all about it," Rachel snapped. "If you don't mind," she said archly, managing to shove Rafe off the blanket as she spoke, "I'd like a little privacy. This bedroom has turned into Grand Central Station." She brushed her sticky hair back off her face with as much dignity as she could muster under the circumstances.

Rafe got to his feet. "Maybe Mr. Welles wants to lay claim to this room too?"

Ned gave Rafe a wily grin, then shifted his gaze back to Rachel. It obviously wasn't the room he was thinking about laying claim to.

CHAPTER THREE

When Rachel came downstairs an hour later, she felt a little more composed and far less exposed dressed in her pleated pale blue trousers and matching oversize silk crepe-de-chine shirt. Ned Welles looked up from the harvest table as she entered the breakfast room. He offered her a cheerful smile, his gaze taking in her new outfit. If he was disappointed with the cover-up, he kept it to himself.

Rachel scanned the room cautiously, then glanced over at the extra cup of coffee at a place setting across from Ned's. "Rafe's?"

"Yours. I heard you coming downstairs, so I poured you a cup. If you drink coffee?" He grinned. "Or is it strictly orange juice?"

Rachel scowled. "Spare me the humor. One comedian in the house is already more than I can cope with."

"Sorry." He gave a contrite smile and extended his hand. "Let's start again. Ned Welles. Pleased to meet you."

Rachel gave his hand a cursory shake and sat down. "Norah's sister, Rachel Mason."

"Yes, I know. Norah talks about you all the time. I've been looking forward to meeting you." He leaned a little closer to her. "You know, Norah told me you were a very beautiful woman. But she was wrong."

Rachel took a sip of the hot, freshly brewed coffee, waiting for the rest of Ned's line. Men like Ned Welles usually had a slick approach when it came to women, as well as to business. More often than not, it was a key to their success. Rachel knew; she had dated her share of the type.

"Beautiful doesn't do you justice," Ned went on after a carefully planned pause. "You're quite extraordinary. A veritable feast for the eyes."

Rachel laughed dryly. "Well, I can't argue that you haven't seen enough of me to know." She ignored Ned's broad, approving smile and took a warm breakfast roll from a wicker basket and began buttering it. "You should be advised that I don't make it a habit of greeting strangers in my bedroom—especially when I happen to be wearing a revealing item of lingerie."

He cocked his head. "Is it a habit reserved for ex-husbands, then?"

Rachel gave him a long, steady look, which she figured was answer enough.

It turned out not to be.

"She does have some strange habits, Welles," Rafe said, breezing into the room. "I ought to warn you." He leaned over Rachel's shoulder and blithely lifted the roll from her plate, taking a bite. Before straightening up, he planted a loud, moist kiss on her cheek.

46

"Good morning, darling," Rafe said airily, his fingers skimming her hair. "Got the orange juice out, I see." He glanced over at Ned Welles. "Another of her amusing habits. Has this absolute passion for orange juice. Only the freshly squeezed kind, I should tell you."

"I am sure," Rachel said stiffly, "that Mr. Welles is not interested in my passions."

Rafe pulled up a chair beside her and took a roll from the basket. "Oh, I think you're wrong, darling." He shot another glance at Ned. "I think he's very interested—in your passions."

"Rafe . . ." Rachel's tone was chilling, but it had no effect on her ex-husband, who was pouring himself a cup of coffee from the carafe on the table. Turning to Ned, he said casually, "She can be irresistible, Welles. But I'd better warn you, she throws a mean left hook and she's subject to tantrums."

"I have no problems with assertive women, Kincaid," Ned replied coolly.

"Are you two finished?" Rachel said fiercely, slamming her half full coffee cup down on the table so that the brown liquid splattered on her shirt as well as Rafe's. However, she was too enraged to care or even notice. "Because if you are, you might let me get in a few words of my own." Her slate-blue eyes turned almost black. She opened her mouth to go on and then abruptly shut it, giving herself a moment to calm down a little. "If I weren't well brought up, which is something I can't say for the two of you," she said in

47

clipped tones, pulling out her seat and standing rigidly erect, "I'd tell you both to . . ." She stepped back, struggling for composure. "Actually, I believe you can fill in the blanks . . . two such clever men as you." With that she swung around and left the room.

The phone started to ring as Rachel stepped into the hall. She picked it up at the same time that Lois got on the line in the kitchen. It was Norah.

"I've got it, Lois," Rachel said crisply.

"Hi. How's everything going?" There was a brief hesitation in Norah's voice as she greeted her sister.

"Oh, things are going swimmingly," Rachel snapped.

"I gather from the tone in your voice that you and Rafe touched base already."

"Why didn't you *tell* me?"

"I just found out." Norah sighed. "When I got into town yesterday, Josh was tied up in business meetings and ended up having to go out of town until this morning, so I didn't get a chance to speak to him until just now. It seems that he'd gotten a call from Rafe yesterday; he'd just flown in from Nicaragua and phoned Josh from New York. Rafe told him he was going to head straight out to the island. It seems he felt bad about missing our wedding and he turned his assignment over to one of his assistants."

"Well, you and Josh rate, anyway. Rafe only barely managed to show up at our own wedding. Actually, he tried to get me to postpone it for some assignment or other. The particulars elude me at the moment."

48

"Rafe did ask Josh on the phone if you would be out there yet, but Josh said you wouldn't be coming until Wednesday or Thursday. I didn't get a chance to tell him you'd called me and were coming out last night. I guess Rafe was as surprised to find you there as you were to find him."

"Let's just say it was a toss-up."

"Did Ned Welles arrive?"

Rachel chuckled dryly. "The man you told me to be charming to? You needn't worry about Mr. Welles, Norah. He has quite enough charm for both of us. In fact, between Rafe and Ned, I'm drowning in attention."

"Rachel, you sound terribly upset about all this. Oh, I know it's a bit of a shock to see Rafe again after all this time, but really, you ought to get a grip on yourself."

"Thank you so much for your sisterly advice, Norah. I shall give it careful consideration," she said rigidly. *"While I'm in the process of going stark raving mad,"* she finished off with a shriek.

Norah was dumbfounded. "Rachel? What is the matter with you? I've never heard you sound so . . . so out of control. You're really beginning to worry me."

Rachel took a deep breath. Norah was right. She was falling apart. She forcefully reminded herself that this was supposed to be a time of prenuptial bliss for her sister and Josh Kincaid. She had no right to spoil

49

it simply because she was faced with an infuriating ex-husband and a new Casanova.

Trying to push aside the fact that she and these two men were going to have to spend days on end under the same roof, Rachel said more civilly, "I'm sorry, Norah. I guess it's the shock of seeing Rafe again. He . . . caught me completely off-guard." She managed a small smile. "So did Ned Welles, as a matter of fact."

"Oh? What exactly do you mean?"

"Just one of those comedy of errors that you don't ever think really happens to anyone. I'll tell you all about it when I see you. When will I see you?"

Norah picked up the hint of desperation in her sister's voice. "Feeling the need for a chaperon, after all?"

"A security guard is more like it."

Norah laughed. "I think you underestimate yourself, little sister. Just pull yourself together. When you're at your fighting best, you never have any difficulties handling matters of the heart. After five years of fending off serious involvements, I'm sure you'll do just fine."

"Well, I'm glad one of us is confident," Rachel said sullenly.

"Anyway, rescue—of sorts—is on the way."

"If you're trying to inspire confidence, Norah Mason, you are not doing a great job."

"I meant that you wouldn't be all alone with those two devilishly handsome men for much longer. Liz Eastman is coming out this afternoon."

"The decorator?"

"Right," Norah said. Once again there was a moment's hesitation before she went on. "It's a little bit awkward, actually."

"Awkward?" Rachel asked warily. "Why is that?"

"Well, it's just that Liz and Ned have dated a few times—more than a few times, actually. For a while there, everyone thought they were going to get married. But something went awry, as they say. They broke up four months ago. When Ellen Kincaid commissioned Liz to do the decorating for the wedding, she didn't realize that Liz knew Ned rather intimately."

"Norah, do you realize what kind of armed camp you're creating here?"

"I'm not too concerned about Liz and Ned. They parted amicably. And Liz didn't seem to mind that Ned was going to be out on the island a good deal of the time she'd be there."

"And Ned? How does he feel about it?" Just then, Rafe came sauntering into the hall. "Hold on a minute, Norah." She gave Rafe a condescending look. "Is there something I can do for you?"

Rafe grinned. "Never ask such a leading question, Rachel."

She sighed wearily. "Listen, Norah, I'll talk to you later."

"I heard all that. I see he hasn't changed very much." Norah laughed softly.

"My thoughts exactly," Rachel said tightly. Her

eyes narrowed on Rafe, who was leaning against the newel post at the bottom of the stairs.

"I'll be out tomorrow, mid-morning," Norah said. "Can I bring you anything?"

"A few grenades, a shotgun . . ."

"I'll see what I can do. Oh, Rachel. About Ned . . ."

"You can tell me about that situation when you come out." After a quick good-bye under Rafe's blatantly watchful eye, Rachel hung up the phone. "Another thing, Rafe Kincaid," she said, picking up on last night's critique of her ex-husband's less than sterling qualities as if no time had passed. "You're still incredibly rude. And I didn't appreciate that snappy little show you put on in the breakfast room. From now on"—she pulled back her shoulders and started up the stairs—"do not call me darling, do not greet me with a kiss, and do not make suggestive references about my habits to the other guests." She marched up the stairs.

"Anything else?" he called up as she stepped onto the next landing.

She tossed him a look over her shoulder. "Yes, as a matter of fact. Don't ever bring me another glass of freshly squeezed orange juice."

She heard Rafe's deep laughter as she headed up to the third floor. As angry as she was feeling, she couldn't help smiling. But the smile faded, and she shook her head, annoyed with herself for allowing Rafe to get her riled so easily. He did seem to bring out the child in her. Not to mention the woman. The heat of that kiss they'd shared up in her room that morning still lingered.

Rachel felt a disturbing twinge as she entered the third-floor bedroom. Lois had not been up yet to make the bed, and the tangled, juice-stained blanket lay on the floor in a crumpled heap. Deliberately ignoring the reminder of her passionate and ultimately hostile struggle with Rafe, Rachel picked up a magazine, one of a pile that Norah had left for her, from a small oak table. She made herself comfortable on a chintzy chaise.

Rachel smiled as she thumbed through the copy of *MS*. If she'd had her own subscription to this bible for the modern, assertive working woman, her membership would have no doubt been revoked after the morning's folly.

She was half dozing, the magazine having fallen to her lap, when there was a light rap on her door. Rachel's eyes sprang open instantly. "I am not thirsty," she said acidly.

The door opened slightly. "I didn't bring you a drink," a throaty, feminine voice replied.

"Oh," Rachel said as the door opened farther. "Sorry. I thought it was Rafe. You must be Liz Eastman."

Liz Eastman had the looks to go with the voice: tall, blond, sophisticated, and patrician-looking, from her smartly coiffed head to her Charles Jordan–clad feet. She wore an expensive, beautifully cut Christian Dior

53

white jersey dress that showed off her slender figure to perfection. Rachel, clad in her coffee-stained, loose-fitting outfit, felt decidedly plain by comparison.

Rachel stood up and smoothed out her pants. The magazine fell to the floor. She caught the tiny smile on Liz's smartly colored lips as she glanced at the magazine title.

"I'm Rachel Mason," Rachel introduced herself, trying to achieve a modicum of grace.

"Yes. I gathered that. Lord, but you don't resemble Norah in the least."

As Liz didn't offer any more on the subject, Rachel had no idea precisely what the remark meant.

"I met your ex-husband downstairs. He was on the phone—to Nigeria or some such place—and he mumbled where you were to me before his party came on the line. Striking-looking man."

While Liz Eastman may have not waxed eloquent on her and Norah, as far as Liz's assessment of Rafe was concerned, he obviously got the decorator's seal of approval. Rachel felt a most disturbing flash of jealousy, then immediately scolded herself for that response. If Liz found Rafe attractive, she was welcome to him. Rachel told herself that she couldn't care less.

"I guess," Liz said hesitantly, "this must be awkward for you." She gave a nod in the general direction of the door. "Having this reunion with your ex?"

"I suppose it's equally awkward for you. Norah told me that you and Ned were once . . . involved."

"The past is the past." Liz tried for a nonchalent

shrug, but it didn't quite come off. Rachel guessed that Liz hadn't buried the past any more successfully than she.

"It just didn't work out," Liz went on. "We're too much alike, I think. We're both very competitive. After a while it grew exhausting always trying to top each other."

"I'm sure it would." After a brief go-around with Rafe this morning, Rachel was already wiped out, although she was honest enough with herself to admit it wasn't only trying to top him that exhausted her. It was equally draining to fend off a stinging attraction for a man she'd thought she'd gotten out of her system years ago.

As if Liz was able to read her mind, she observed, "I would guess it wouldn't be easy to forget a man like Rafe Kincaid, especially after having been married to him."

"It was a short marriage. Time dims all memories." Rachel applauded herself for her bravura performance. However, she was eager to get off the topic. "So tell me, Liz, what plans do you have in mind for Norah's wedding?"

Liz didn't seem disappointed by the change in subject matter. "I've brought along scads of drawings and swatches. You'll have to come down and have a look." She paused for a moment. "I understand you used Wilma Gilberte as the decorator for your wedding here on the island."

"Yes." Rachel thought about the stout, French,

middle-aged designer who seemed to get everything done without anyone noticing she was even around. She found herself wishing that Ellen Kincaid had opted to use her again. Unlike Wilma Gilberte, Liz was nothing if not highly visible. Rachel had a feeling that with Liz here, the sparks already set in motion would have a veritable field day.

"Wilma's tastes ran to the more traditional," Liz said. "To be frank, I think she lacks creative spirit. If you want to make a splash in this business, you have to take risks. I always take risks if I think they'll pay off."

"I thought Wilma did a delightful job on the house for my wedding," Rachel said tartly. "It was warm, tasteful, really quite splendid."

"I agree."

Both women's eyes shot to the open door where Rafe was standing, smoking a cigarette, leaning against the jamb. "The house looked great for our wedding," he went on. "A perfect backdrop for the blushing bride."

"And the blushing groom?" Liz inquired with a saucy little smile.

"The groom wasn't the blushing type." He grinned, dousing his cigarette in an ashtray on the entry table.

"Did you want something, Rafe?" Rachel swallowed hard. There she was, giving him a perfect opening again for a taunting response. "I mean, why are you standing at my door again?" she quickly

56

amended, realizing as she did that she was only making matters worse.

Rafe took in her embarrassment with apparent pleasure. "I came up to tell Miss Eastman that there's a phone call for her."

"Oh, that's probably the fabric shop," Liz said, hurrying out.

Rafe, on the other hand, appeared to be in no hurry at all to leave.

Rachel gave him a critical gaze, then cast her eyes over to the phone on her bedside table. "I didn't hear it ring." Her tone was accusatory.

"You think I used the phone call as an excuse to be alone with you?"

"Did you?" she asked acidly.

He stared at her with a silent appraisal. Then, without a word, he walked across the room to the table by the bed and lifted up the phone from which an unconnected wire dangled. "Shall I plug it in for you? It will save you—"

"From making a fool of myself?" Rachel lowered her eyes. "Maybe you'd better," she said softly.

Rafe smiled. For the first time that cutting edge seemed to be missing. "I was going to say, save you from mistrusting my every word." He pulled the table out, bent down, and plugged the wire into the jack.

Rachel was acutely aware of his well-muscled thighs, the thin material of his chinos taut against his skin as he bent. When he stood up, she hastily averted her gaze.

"That's taken care of," he said pleasantly.

"Thanks."

He looked out the window. "The rain is still coming down."

"Is it?" she asked inanely, watching his face uncertainly, his presence stirring up longings once again. It was even harder now because the aggressive glint in his eyes was gone. Suddenly he seemed a bit awkward, himself, which was remarkable, since his earlier comment to Liz had been accurate. He was as far removed from being a blushing groom as a man could be. Blushing ex-groom, she hastened to correct herself. Nothing ever seemed to ruffle him.

Rafe continued looking out the window. "Remember how we used to love to take walks on the island on days like this? You'd put on that funny oversize yellow slicker and those crazy galoshes my Great-Aunt Laura gave you?"

Rachel smiled. "I hadn't seen a pair of real honest-to-goodness galoshes since I was a little girl. She was a dear, your Great-Aunt Laura."

"She was very fond of you. I remember she called me aside right before the ceremony—" he stopped abruptly.

Rachel saw him shrug.

"It was a long time ago," he said in a low voice. He turned his gaze to her, studying her for a long moment before speaking again. "There were times over these past few years that our marriage felt like some kind of a dream . . . a fantasy that only lived in my imagina-

58

tion. I'd be off in the Middle East or on some assignment in South America, and all of a sudden I'd find myself wondering if you ever really did exist. Strange, isn't it?"

Rachel shook her head slowly. "No," she said in a low voice, "it isn't strange. I had those same feelings on occasion." She looked away. "Being back here on the island . . . seeing you again after all these years . . . well"—she smiled wistfully—"it makes our past seem very vivid and real."

He swung around to her. "Let's go take a walk, Rachel. I bet we can still dig up those galoshes and that slicker. We can head down to the cove, see who comes up with the funniest-looking piece of driftwood. Remember the one I found that summer that looked like the face of a pig?"

"With its snout sawed off." Rachel laughed.

"Come on. Let's go exploring. You know how I hate being cooped up."

Until that last remark Rachel had all but made up her mind to join him. The problem was, she remembered only too well how much Rafe hated being confined. In one of their most heated fights he'd accused her of just that—trying to keep him cooped up.

"Rachel . . ."

"I don't think so, Rafe. I didn't come back to the island to reminisce or to relive happier times. Those times are over. We made that choice together."

The hard lines returned to Rafe's face. "Did we?" His tone was low and accusing.

"Yes," Rachel said firmly. "We did." She turned away. "The past may not be a figment of our imagination, Rafe, but it isn't a reality I ever care to relive."

"You have a strange way, Rachel, of turning the simplest gesture into a major statement of intent. I was suggesting a walk, not a resurrection of our marriage. Believe me, that's the last thing in the world I'd want to live through again." He walked toward her, stopping less than a foot away. "These past five years have been great for me. I never knew how precious freedom was until that divorce decree came through. I should never have married you, Rachel. In a way I blame our marriage on your youth. If you hadn't been so damn innocent and inexperienced six years ago in Senegal, I simply would have taken you to bed a few times and very likely discovered it was quite enough. It would have saved us both a lot of grief."

Livid with rage, she gave him an icy glare. "You could save us both a lot of grief from here on out if you'd simply leave me alone. This is supposed to be a magical, romantic time for Josh and Norah. We can't let our personal feelings ruin it in any way for them. So let's both try to act grown-up, Rafe. Let's put on cheery smiles and pretend we are having a reasonably pleasant, mature reunion. Surely a man of your years and vast experience ought to be able to pull that off with ease."

Rafe grinned. "I'm not so sure, Rachel. You seem to bring out the child in me."

"The beast is more like it," she muttered.

"Uh-uh, Rachel. You aren't setting a very good example."

"Rafe, I mean it. We can't be constantly bickering with each other. It wouldn't be fair to Norah and Josh."

Rafe nodded. "Okay, Rachel. Truce. On one condition."

She eyed him warily.

"Let's not just pretend to be civil. Let's actually try to do it for real. You can start by taking that walk with me."

"And how do you start?"

Rafe smiled. "I start by digging up those old galoshes for you."

Rachel felt a tingling sensation travel down her spine as his eyes held hers. Here she was on shaky ground again and she couldn't even figure out how it had happened. Instead of trying, she managed a faint smile and a brief nod.

CHAPTER FOUR

The yellow slicker had managed to disappear over the years, but Rafe produced the old galoshes for Rachel and dug up another equally tattered slicker from one of the downstairs' closets.

Rachel did a heavy-footed pirouette in the hallway. "Classy, don't you think?"

Rafe smiled softly. "Absolutely."

It wasn't the reaction Rachel had expected. "Hey, this is your chance to get in a good laugh."

Before Rafe could answer, Ned Welles strolled into the hall from the living room. He gave Rachel a perplexed look. "Where are you off to in this storm?"

"Oh, it's not a storm," Rachel said. "Just a shower."

Rafe was slipping a black nylon rain parka over his head. "A little water never hurt anyone, Welles."

"I'm not so sure," Liz Eastman said, coming down the stairs. "People have been known to drown in water." A broad smile broke across her face. "I'd hate to see that happen to you." Her statement seemed to take in Rafe alone.

"I'll make sure we avoid all large raindrops," Rachel declared.

"Well, in that case maybe I'll join you," Ned said. He shot a quick glance at Liz. "I could use a breath of fresh air myself."

Rachel caught the arch tone in his voice, the harsh glint in otherwise warm brown eyes. So, she thought, Ned wasn't any more blasé about Liz's presence as she was of his.

"What about you, Liz?" Rafe asked. "Shall we make it a foursome?"

Liz shook her head. "No thanks. Unlike the rest of you, I'm here to work. Besides, I abhor walks in the rain. I prefer operating on dry ground."

"I'll just run upstairs," Ned said tautly, "and get a raincoat. I'll only be a minute."

Rafe took hold of Rachel's elbow. "We'll wait outside for you."

As soon as they'd stepped out the door, Rachel found herself, much to her astonishment, being lifted over Rafe's shoulder.

"What are you doing?" she shouted. "Put me down."

But Rafe ignored her protests and her thrashing, and dashed across the lawn toward the large, stone, four-car garage.

"Rafe—"

"There are a lot of puddles here, Rachel. Just trying to see to it that you don't go and drown on me." He hoisted her more solidly on his shoulder despite her

63

attempts to be released. He scooted around to the back of the large, two-story building.

"This is a cruel prank to play on Ned, Rafe," she snapped.

Rafe finally let her slip down off him but kept his arms around her. Rachel found herself pressed tightly against him.

"I find Ned a bore," Rafe said blithely. "Anyway, I always did hate guys who invite themselves along when they're not wanted."

"Well, I think you're being absolutely rude. Now let go of me and let me find him," she demanded, raindrops splashing on her face as she tilted her head to meet his gaze.

She heard Ned's voice from the distance calling out to them. Rachel opened her mouth to answer him, but before she could, Rafe's face descended, and he kissed her with a passion that took her breath away. The kiss was long and slow, melting her resistance.

He lifted his face from hers slightly. "If you attempt to answer Welles, I'll be forced to do that again, Rachel." His husky voice vibrated against her lips, and his arms were tight around her waist, making her body arch against his. Despite the cool rain beating down on them, Rachel felt heated.

"And if I agree," she murmured breathlessly, "to keep quiet?"

His thumb moved tantalizingly across her lower lip. "I'm afraid you're in one of those no-win situations."

"Oh . . ." Her fingers curved around his neck, and

a groan rose from her throat as Rafe's tongue plunged deep into her mouth. She offered no struggle as he pressed her hard against him, making her stunningly aware of his sharp arousal in spite of the layers of clothing between them. If Ned Welles was still calling, she didn't even hear him.

Her hood fell down over her shoulders, and Rafe's fingers raked through her hair. She followed his move. Rafe's thick, dark hair was already soaking wet since he'd not bothered with his own hood, and the feel of it against her own fingers brought back torrid memories —like the time Rafe had come home from an assignment earlier than expected. She had been in the middle of a shower. He'd stepped right in with her, fully dressed, and Rachel had taken great relish in stripping the drenched clothes from his body so, as she'd laughingly whispered, they'd be equals.

Rachel moved to disentangle herself from his embrace. "We're taking civility a bit too far," she said in a faltering voice.

Rafe sighed, releasing her without protest. "You're right. Let's walk."

She gave him a surreptitious glance, disconcerted to see that the hard glint had abruptly returned to his blue eyes. They walked side by side, a safe distance between them, Rafe unusually quiet.

Rachel didn't understand his silence. For a brief time, when they were first married, she'd actually thought she was beginning to figure Rafe out. But she soon discovered that so much about her husband was unfathomable, at least to her. For all they'd shared together, there was a solitary quality about Rafe; he seemed so self-contained. She knew he'd wanted her, but never, during the whole time they were together, had she felt he truly needed her. That realization always saddened her.

The sadness clung to her now as she walked beside Rafe. He seemed lost in his own private thoughts, thoughts that he didn't choose to share with her. She shivered.

"Are you cold?"

"No," she said sharply.

He looked over at her curiously, saying nothing.

"It must have been harrowing in Nicaragua," she said quietly.

If Rafe had any feelings about her change of topic, he gave no sign.

"Tough assignment. There were a few hairy times. But that's all part of the game."

"Game?" Her tone was disapproving.

A wry smile flickered across Rafe's face. "I've always found that the best way to view what I do. If you take the danger too seriously, you'll end up backing off. A good photojournalist never backs off."

What about a good husband? She wanted to ask, but she kept the question to herself.

She caught him smiling at her. "I guess we lost sight of the playful aspects of our marriage," he said, as if reading her mind. "When things grew deadly serious between us—"

"You fled," she finished acerbically.

"We both fled, Rachel," he said firmly, gripping her elbow and forcing her to come to an abrupt halt. "As long as our marriage was a game, we could play it out beautifully. But as soon as the rules got changed—"

"You mean, you think I changed the rules," she accused. "Why not just say it, Rafe? Be honest for once in your life."

The line of Rafe's mouth was tight, and the muscles along his jawline tensed. "Why is it we can't seem to spend more than five minutes together without either bickering or falling prey to pure lust, Rachel?"

"I'd be very happy to do without both." She eyed him defiantly, daring him to contradict her.

Instead he broke into soft laughter. "Oh, Rachel," he finally said, with a sigh, "you still provoke me like no other woman. Something tells me, the same is true for you. Or have there been other men?"

"Men who provoke me, or men in my life in general?" she quipped.

He studied her thoughtfully. "Josh tells me you've become all work and no play."

"Josh does not know the details of my personal life. He and Norah both seem to think that just because I've become modestly successful and put in long hours that my love life has suffered terribly." She gave him a quick glance. "You're certainly successful, and there's no one who would say you don't put in grueling hours. But I'm sure you still find time for . . . a private life."

He smiled broadly. "Is that a statement or a question?"

They were approaching the cove, the rain now no more than a tiny trickle. Rachel bent down and picked up a small piece of driftwood, holding it out. "What do you think?" Then she tossed it away. "No, not a prizewinner."

"Okay, so we won't talk about our personal involvements—or lack of them—of the past five years," Rafe said lightly, pulling his jacket up over his head.

Rachel slipped off the galoshes, letting her bare feet sink into the cool, wet sand, then undid her slicker. Rafe took it from her and dropped it along with his to the ground.

"The sun's coming out." He grinned at her. "See, the day isn't a lost cause, after all."

Rachel looked out across the cove to a smaller island that also belonged to the Kincaid family. Gerald Kincaid, Rafe's father, had bought that island as a young man. With his own two hands he'd built a small, quaint cottage on it where he and Ellen used to spend their summers until Josh was born. Then he purchased the larger island across the cove with the grand, stone manor house. Over the years the small cottage had deteriorated from disuse.

The summer that Rachel and Rafe spent on Kincaid Island, they often sailed across to the smaller isle. They'd even fixed the cottage up a little, choosing to spend some nights there so they could be alone when guests descended on the main island.

Rafe followed Rachel's gaze. "I wonder what the old place looks like these days. Josh told me that Dad's thinking of tearing the cottage down. His brother, Leon, wants to buy the island and put up one of those sleek, modern, glass monstrosities for one of his daughters."

Rachel couldn't hide the sad look in her eyes. "What a pity. . . ."

Rafe glanced over at the motorized sailboat moored on the beach. "Let's go over and have a look. It could be our last chance."

Rachel hesitated. How many more old memories could she handle in one day? But Rafe's hand was pressed against her back, urging her forward. "Come on, Rachel." He held a hand up, Boy Scout fashion. "No bickering, I promise."

She noted, as she allowed him to help her climb into the boat, that he omitted any promise about "no lust." She decided to keep that observation to herself.

Rather than relying on the wind, Rafe started the outboard engine. It took a few tries. As he attended to the motor Rachel's eyes kept drifting to Rafe's strong, deeply tanned arms. Beneath the thin material of his jersey she could make out the outline of his broad chest, wide shoulders, and hard, muscled stomach.

When he finally managed to start the engine, he wiped sweat from his brow. The sky had cleared, and a brilliant late-morning sun shone down on them. Rafe casually removed his jersey, revealing his rippled muscles. Rachel averted her gaze, sitting primly on the side of the boat.

Rafe turned off the motor when they were halfway to the tiny island. "Let's take a swim," he said casually. "It's getting hot."

"I—I didn't wear a suit."

Rafe shrugged. "We've gone skinny-dipping before." He saw Rachel's deepening scowl. "Okay, so we won't go in the buff. Look, you're wearing a bra and panties under that outfit, aren't you? And I've got on a pair of briefs underneath my slacks. They're less revealing than those skimpy bathing suits we would have worn if we'd come dressed for a swim."

Rachel had to admit that was true. The two bikinis she'd brought along for her two-week stay on the island were scant, to say the least. And she was very warm. Still, she hesitated. Whether or not Rafe was sincere about keeping lust at bay, she was determined not to get caught up in new games.

"No, I really don't want to go swimming," she said archly.

Rafe stood up and blithely undid his trousers. "Suit yourself." He stepped out of his pants, folded them casually, and placed them on one of the benches. As he perched on the edge of the boat, his back to her, Rachel's eyes traveled with a hungry curiosity over the muscled length of his legs to the scant strip of tight black briefs across his flexed buttocks, up over the ridged notches of his darkly tanned back. As he dived into the sea Rachel allowed a gasp to escape her

70

throat. Unconsciously her hand moved to her breast. She could feel both the rapid pounding of her heart and the even more disconcerting hardening of her nipple.

Rafe swam with strong, easy strides, his dark head surfacing, disappearing, and resurfacing again. Rachel knew he expected her to give in and join him in the water. Why shouldn't he? She had always acquiesced in the past. But stubbornness was one of her newly acquired attributes, one that Rafe had not been around to watch develop these past five years. Stubbornness and a determination to set her own terms.

She did unfasten the bottom buttons of her shirt, tying the ends in a knot to cool off her midriff. And she rolled her slacks up to her knees, making every effort to ignore the cloying dampness of perspiration that made her clothes stick to her body.

Rafe grabbed hold of the side of the boat, flicking cold water into Rachel's face. She gave him a contemptuous look. "Are we going over to have a look at the cottage or not?"

He grinned. "What ever happened to your spirit of adventure, Rachel?"

"I never had a spirit of adventure. I was simply a starry-eyed kid determined to prove to you that I could hold my own in the worst of circumstances."

"I don't believe you."

"It's true."

"Any more than I believe you really want to sit

there sweltering in the hot August sun when you could jump into this cool, inviting water."

"Believe whatever you like," Rachel said archly.

"You do make things difficult for yourself, Rachel."

She screamed as he caught her around the waist. "Don't you dare—"

A few moments later, when she surfaced from the water in a fury, she began swatting at his dodging, laughing figure.

"It isn't funny," she shouted, trying to tread water while she shrieked and punched out toward him.

"Come on, Rachel. This is my chance to have that good laugh you promised me."

"Oh, so you want a good laugh, do you?" she muttered, shaking water from her hair as she hoisted herself onto the boat—not an easy task in her sodden clothes.

Rafe was still chuckling as Rachel started the motor. He caught on to the side again, but as he started to climb in, Rachel pried his fingers open and gave him a hefty shove. "You had your laugh, Rafe Kincaid. Now it's my turn to have one. Let's see who can make it to the island first," she called out as the boat began to take off.

"Rachel, get back here. Are you crazy?"

"Where's your spirit of adventure, Kincaid?" she yelled as she waved cheerily.

Before she got too far, she tossed a life preserver over the boat, although she doubted he'd use it. She knew he'd sooner drown than concede that he was in need of any assistance.

She was sitting on a grassy dune at the edge of the beach when Rafe, without the life preserver, dragged himself out of the water. He stretched flat down on the sand. After a couple of minutes of catching his breath he lifted his head and glared at Rachel, who was twenty feet away.

"I could have drowned," he rasped.

"Maybe we should have heeded Liz's warning," Rachel quipped.

"Very amusing." He gave her a contemptuous look. "I ought to tan your hide for that little stunt."

"That would be grounds for divorce . . . if we weren't already divorced, of course."

"You've turned very callous and vindictive since becoming a divorcee, Rachel Kincaid."

"That's Rachel Mason." She grinned. "And I wasn't being callous. I did throw you that life preserver. If you weren't so hung up on your tough-guy image, you wouldn't have had to work so hard." She paused. Then, putting aside the teasing banter, she said soberly, "You never could take a helping hand from anyone, Rafe. That was another one of your problems. You had to go it alone. I'm amazed you actually turned the Nicaragua assignment over to one of your assistants. You wouldn't have done that in the old days."

"She's good. One of the few female photojournalists I can trust." He rolled over onto his back, his eyes cast skyward. "One of the few women I can trust, as a matter of fact."

"How nice for you," she said evenly. Unable to maintain a facade of indifference about that tidbit of news, she quickly rose to her feet and turned toward the cottage.

"She doesn't have a vindictive bone in her body. And she doesn't get her kicks from pulling sneaky, childish stunts."

"That's great," Rachel shouted back venomously as she marched up the path.

"And," Rafe said, getting to his feet and heading after her, "she isn't a goddamn tease. She doesn't play come-and-get-it and then slam the door in your face."

Rachel pulled up short and whirled around to face him. "You're accusing me of being a . . . tease. Talk about the pot calling the kettle black."

Rafe grinned. "I'm more than willing to finish anything I start, Rachel. You're the one sending mixed signals."

Rage engulfed her. "How dare you accuse me . . ." She swallowed convulsively. "You've made all the moves here, Rafe Kincaid. And," she said, glaring at him, "since you've brought up the subject, just what is the seduction bit all about? Don't tell me you still need to prove your sexual prowess with a cast-off wife. Can't pass up a chance to make a conquest even with old news? Or is it just a need to get back at me, Rafe?"

"Get back at you for what?" he said, taunting her. "For doing me the biggest favor of my life? Let's face

74

it, Rachel, it was only a matter of time. We were traveling down rocky byways right from the start. You just hit the fork in the road and veered off on your own a few miles before I did." He brushed past her and headed up the path.

"So why are you coming on to me, Rafe Kincaid? You answer me that," she shouted after him.

"Call it . . . unfinished business," he bellowed back.

"We don't have any unfinished business." She raced up to him, grabbing hold of his arm. She pulled him to a stop. "We have a divorce decree to prove it," she argued, watching Rafe's eyes travel down the length of her, aware of how bedraggled she looked. She let go of him, protectively hugging her arms around her chest. "You could have put your clothes back on," she muttered.

He glanced down at his own body as if realizing his state of undress for the first time. He laughed softly. "You could have been kind enough to bring them out of the boat for me."

"I'm not kind. I'm vindictive, callous, untrustworthy. Now, I'm sure your little assistant would have been ever so much more thoughtful."

"Add jealousy to that list of your winning qualities," he said with a wink. "I'll grab my clothes and meet you up at the cottage. After all, I wouldn't want to tantalize you beyond endurance."

"Don't flatter yourself."

When Rachel got to the cottage, she felt a wave of

sadness as she saw how much more the building had deteriorated over the past five years. Several roof shingles lay on the ground, and a couple of shutters hung by little more than a thread. The warm, gray, weathered cedar clapboard now looked weatherbeaten. The door, which Rachel herself had painted a warm, inviting cherry red six summers ago, looked tawdry and unwelcoming now that it had faded to a dull purple.

She hesitated at the door, opening it slowly. The Kincaids never locked it, as they'd never had any problem with vandals and there wasn't anything of value inside the house to take. The hinges creaked loudly.

Rachel stepped inside and looked around the small, cozy living room with its hand-hewn posts and beams. She smiled. The inside had aged better than the outside. It was stuffy and dusty, but otherwise was little changed from the past. She opened the windows, then walked idly around the room running her hand lightly over the oak fireplace mantel, decorated with a stenciled flower design, the faded chintz couch, the wicker rocker with the lacquer finish she'd helped Rafe apply. The old clock she and Rafe had dug up in the basement of the stone house was still resting on the cherrywood breakfront. She looked around for the key to wind it up, but it was nowhere in sight.

"No turning back the time," she said aloud in a wistful voice.

Rafe stepped onto the porch. He was wearing his

trousers, but he hadn't bothered with his shirt. He tossed it on an old ash entry table as he stepped inside.

"The outside's in a sad state, but it's not too bad in here," he said, echoing Rachel's sentiments.

She wandered into the small kitchen. Pulling out an old dishcloth from one of the drawers, she wiped the inside of a big picture window next to which she and Rafe used to eat most of their meals. "Pretty grimy," she commented idly, hearing his footsteps as he entered the room.

"Yeah, pretty grimy." He turned, his footsteps fading.

A few minutes later he called out to her. "Hey, come into the bedroom."

Rachel arched a brow. "What for?"

He didn't answer.

"Rafe . . ." She walked into the living room. "Damn," she muttered.

"Look," he said, appearing at the bedroom door. He was holding up a pale yellow sundress. "You always looked beautiful in this dress." He smiled. "I thought you might like to change out of those damp clothes."

"I didn't realize I'd left any of my clothes here."

"There are some other things too."

For a moment Rachel imagined she heard a catch in his voice. She tilted her head. "What kinds of things?"

Rachel hesitated for a moment and then entered. It was a small, pretty, blue-and-white-flowered room with a large brass-and-white-metal bed covered with an old handmade quilt. There was a faded shag rug on the wide pine floor, an oak writing desk in the corner, and a narrow, slightly crooked bookcase beside it.

Rafe pushed away the curtains and opened the windows. He looked out at the water as Rachel walked slowly over to the bed. Tears stung her eyes as she stared up at the bouquet of pressed flowers set behind glass and hung over the headboard on the wall. Her wedding bouquet.

Rafe turned around finally. "Rachel . . ."

He walked up behind her, resting his hands on her shoulders. Slowly he pivoted her around. She didn't want him to see the tears, but she couldn't resist the pull of his hands. He leaned down, tenderly kissing both her eyes. He smoothed back her tangled hair and put a finger under her chin. She looked up at him. He pressed his lips to hers for a mere breath of a kiss.

"It wasn't all hell, Rachel." His voice was gentle as he drew her into his arms.

"No," she whispered against his warm skin. "It wasn't all hell."

CHAPTER FIVE

Rachel felt a sudden ache of loneliness well up in her as Rafe's arms enclosed her. It was a feeling she hadn't experienced with such intensity for a long time, but it felt frighteningly familiar nonetheless. For months after their marriage dissolved, Rachel had ached like this. Sometimes she felt she would go mad with the pain. Thank God for the TV show, for the funny, crazy, makeshift family it created for her. The loneliness had eased. But now it was all coming back to her, like a glimpse of what was to come if she was foolish enough to lose her head . . . not to mention her heart.

She pressed her palms against Rafe's bare chest, gently but firmly pushing him away. "Hey," she said softly, "you're forgetting the rules. No bickering . . . and no lust."

He smiled beguilingly. "It isn't exactly lust. Not pure lust, anyway."

"Close enough," she said with more conviction.

He ran a hand lightly down her arm and then stepped away. "I do want you, Rachel. You're still irresistible."

"Don't forget the caution signs that go with that irresistibility. Take one, take it all."

A sudden charged tension filled the air. There was challenge in her deep blue eyes, a challenge that Rafe was not at all prepared to meet. Instead he walked to the bedroom door. "I just might need to take another dip in the cold, cold sea."

His touch of humor softened the strain. Rachel cocked her head. "How about directing your . . . energies toward finding us something to eat instead? Do you suppose there are any canned goods still around?"

"My mother used to see to it that there was always some stuff around, even though anyone rarely came over. We can have a look and see if she's replenished the larder." He hesitated. "Coming?"

"I think I'll throw on the sundress you dug up," she said, walking over to the chair where Rafe had set it down. She lifted it. "A bit out-of-date but dry."

When Rachel entered the kitchen a few minutes later, Rafe was squatting on his knees, his head lost in the cupboard as he rummaged among the canned goods. "Let's see. There's some soup, tuna, sardines, anchovies, and a couple of cans of macaroni and cheese. Well, will you look here. There's even a bottle of vino." His head emerged from under the counter, one hand clasping the wine.

"Not a bad year for . . ." He stopped in mid-sentence and rose to his feet. "Well . . . don't you look . . . pretty."

She smiled, feeling suddenly very shy in the thin

cotton halter dress that hugged her waist, then dropped from her hips into a soft dirndl. Her hands went up to her chest. "It's a little tighter than it was when I first wore it."

"You were . . . still a girl then, Rachel. Now you're very much a woman. For such a delicate creature you're quite voluptuous."

She flushed, then laughed softly. "Why is it when you tell me I'm a child, I feel like a righteous adult, and when you tell me I'm a woman, I feel like a . . . blushing schoolgirl?"

"It's one of those mysteries about you that makes you so intriguing."

She walked over and lifted up the bottle of wine, trying to ignore the new ache assailing her—a hungry, forbidden ache of raw desire.

"You're right," she said, giving the bottle careful scrutiny. "It's not a bad year for Cabernet Sauvignon. I'll make up some soup and open the wine. Okay?"

"Yeah, okay."

"Why don't you go outside and—"

"Take an ice-cold dip in the sea?" He gave her an unnerving smile.

Rachel moved around him to get to the cupboard. She knelt down. "Chicken noodle or minestrone? Oh, not chicken noodle. You hate chicken." Her voice wavered. "Or don't you anymore?"

"Why should that change about me, as in your estimation nothing else has changed?"

Rachel looked up at him, trying to decide if he'd

meant the remark sarcastically. She wasn't sure. *"Have* you changed, Rafe?"

He met her gaze. "Some things have changed. Others endure. I like to think I've gotten a bit wiser as I've grown older. But to be honest, there are times when I think that hasn't happened."

"Like now?" Rachel's voice trembled.

"It isn't very wise to want to make love to you, is it?" He reached out and took hold of her arm. He lifted her to her feet, taking the can of soup from her hand and setting it on the counter. "Is it, Rachel?"

"No . . . it isn't very wise for either one of us."

"Then again," he said in a low, seductive voice, "you're all grown-up now. You can't still require a wedding ring on your finger before you go to bed with a man."

Rachel stiffened. "I require more . . . than you could ever give," she said coldly, wrenching herself free. "I'm hungry. I'm going to make the soup." She ignored his presence as she busily set about finding a can opener and a pot. Rafe watched her for a minute or two, then sullenly searched a drawer for a corkscrew. Finding one, he opened the wine and poured himself a glass. He took it outside onto the porch.

Ten minutes later Rachel brought two bowls of soup outside, along with a glass for herself and the bottle of wine. She set the tray on a white wicker table and pulled up one of the matching wicker chairs.

"Do you want the soup?" she asked in a formal tone, sitting down.

Rafe finished the last swallow of wine and pulled his own chair up to the table. He lifted the wine bottle, pouring a refill for himself and a new glass for Rachel.

They ate in silence for a few minutes. "We should get back after we finish. Ned and Liz might be worried about what became of us," she said finally, uncomfortably aware of his lingering gaze.

"I'm sorry, Rachel."

She took a sip of wine, saw that her hand was trembling, and hoped that Rafe didn't notice. "Sorry about what?"

"Not keeping to our bargain," he said, his tone suddenly flip.

Rachel frowned.

"No . . . not just that," he said in a gentler voice. "I'm sorry about that wedding-ring crack. I guess that's another thing about me that hasn't changed. I still have a rotten temper, and I strike out when I'm mad."

"And when you're hurt," Rachel murmured.

His eyes narrowed. "Maybe so."

"I'm sorry, too, Rafe. It's just . . . I don't want to be hurt again like before. I've put that pain behind me."

"There are never guarantees. Just like there's really no such thing as promises that never get broken."

She smiled wanly. "Yes, I know that much."

"So what's left?" This time there was no flippancy in his tone.

Rachel's slate-blue eyes were shadowed. "Love."

She took another sip of wine for courage. "That's what's left. That's what's important to me. Not meaningless games or a quick roll in the hay or having sex for old times' sake."

She pushed the barely touched soup away and stood up. But as she moved, Rafe snaked out his hand and caught her arm. "Damn it, stop running from me," he said angrily.

"I'm not running. It's just . . . I'm tired of these pointless conversations."

"Sit down and eat."

"I'm not hungry."

He tugged her hard. "I said, sit down."

She couldn't fight the pressure of his downward pull and was forced to comply with his command.

"That's better," he said coolly.

Rachel made no move. He ignored her and began eating his soup.

"You're making a big mistake. You hardly ate anything for breakfast. If you don't watch out, you'll start getting light-headed." He leaned toward her. "And who knows what you might do then?"

Her stomach growled, as if on cue. She pressed her hand against it, ignoring Rafe's grin.

"I get the message, Rachel," he said in between swallows of soup. "You're as stubborn as a she-cat. Now that you've proved your point, eat up your soup before it gets cold." He took another spoonful and popped it into his mouth.

Rachel ran her tongue over dry lips. This was ridiculous. She was ravenous; maybe it was from all that energy she'd used fending off Rafe, fending off her own unbidden desires. But whatever the cause, it was positively idiotic to allow Rafe to make her feel that by eating her lunch he would somehow come out victorious. Resolutely she picked up the spoon in front of her and took a taste of the now tepid soup.

They finished the meal in silence. When they were done, she gathered the dishes and the empty wine bottle onto the tray.

Rafe leaned against the porch railing as he watched her walk into the house. His eyes lingered on her bare back, thinking of the feel of her satiny skin; her sumptuous body; her full, luscious breasts; her slender waist; the subtle swing of her shapely hips as she walked. When he'd decided to come back to the States for his brother's wedding, Rafe knew it would stir some feelings seeing Rachel again for the first time in five years. He was afraid that she'd still look the same, that he would feel the same burgeoning desire stirred by her innocent beauty.

He was wrong. Rachel wasn't the same; her guileless loveliness was gone. But it had been replaced by a far more womanly beauty. And it was not only her looks that had blossomed; so had her spirit. Rachel had become a spellbinding spitfire that Rafe, though he raged against it, found utterly compelling. She was more his match than ever before. And Rafe found that realization more worrisome than all his earlier fears.

When Rachel came outside again, she was carrying

her other clothes and Rafe's shirt over her arm. "Let's head back," she said matter-of-factly.

Rafe nodded, a sudden anger welling up. It infuriated him that Rachel had this mesmerizing power over him, a power that made his body constantly tense with arousal, his heartbeat start racing, and his mind begin inventing the most erotic scenes.

He started down the steps ahead of her, impatient with himself, impatient with her. Why the hell had he changed his mind and come home for Josh's wedding?

Rachel, unable to keep pace with his swiftly changing moods, hesitated on the porch.

"Well, are you coming?" he gritted through clenched teeth.

"Absolutely," she answered tartly, hurrying down the stairs. She was certainly as eager as Mr. Rafe Kincaid to get off this island.

But when they arrived down at the beach, they discovered that there was no boat in sight.

"Where the hell is it?" she demanded.

"I could ask you the same question," he countered with a sneering glance. "You were the one that beached the damn thing. Don't you know how to secure a boat?"

"I pulled it up on the sand, for your information. It was fine when I left it."

"You obviously didn't secure it well enough. The tide must have come in and the boat must have been washed out."

Rachel opened her mouth to deny his statement but

realized that he was probably right. So she glared at him sullenly instead, then started across the narrow beach front in a futile effort to spot the vanished boat.

"Now what?" she said breathlessly as she returned to Rafe minutes later.

"You tell me," he said blithely, stretching out on the sand.

"Don't just lie there. Do something! Maybe there's a rowboat around. Or a canoe."

"Nope."

"How can you be so sure?"

Rafe shrugged. "Go have yourself a look."

"I will. And if I find one, I have a mind to leave you stranded here. Especially as I know damn well that this was all your doing."

He grabbed her ankle as she took a step, forcing her face down in the sand.

"Let go of me," she said sputtering, rubbing sand from her mouth. "I'm sick and tired of you manhandling me."

"And I'm sick and tired," he said in a low, threatening voice as he moved up toward her on the sand and pinned her arms down, "of being made out the heavy all the time. You think if I really wanted to keep you here for a while, I would have needed to resort to a stupid stunt like letting the boat drift off to sea?" He wrenched her over onto her back and moved on top of her, once more pinning her wrists the moment her arms flailed out.

"You know damn well I could have gotten you into

bed if I'd put a little more effort into it," he snapped harshly, trying to ignore the pulsating tension of her body beneath him, the rise and fall of her full breasts, the movement of her hips as she struggled to free herself. "But it wasn't worth the effort," he said in a clipped, curt tone.

"I wouldn't make love to you if you were—"

"The last man on this island?" He grinned suddenly.

She couldn't breathe. Nor could she succumb to pure rage, not with Rafe's body crushing the length of hers, his hot breath ruffling her hair, his eyes staring at her with a disconcerting mixture of amusement and desire.

"The last man on earth," she said with a venomous gasp.

His smile turned rueful. "You could do worse. Take Ned Welles . . ."

"I just might," she said derisively.

"Oh, so that's your type these days, is it?" He pressed down more fully on top of her, his fingers tight around her slender wrists, high over her head. He felt a twinge of guilt, knowing exactly where he was leading this fight, knowing that he wanted her more than he ever had, knowing that Rachel wanted him just as fiercely, knowing, finally, that there was no way either one of them would willingly admit it without the fight.

"Get off me, Rafe."

"I don't think Ned is your type, Rachel. I think he's

much too tame for you." His mouth was close to her ear.

"I like men who don't behave like animals," she hissed.

"Then why are you so aroused right now?" He lifted himself off her only far enough to reveal her taut nipples bursting against the thin cotton halter of her sundress.

"You're disgusting," she spat out, managing to finally wrench one hand free and land it square across his face with a resounding smack.

"Are we down to an eye for an eye?" he asked coldly.

Rachel flinched. "Don't you dare . . ."

It looked to Rachel as if he were carefully considering the possibility, but he finally rolled off her onto the sand.

She took a deep breath and let the tension slowly subside in her body.

Rafe pressed an arm over his eyes to block out the sun. He was sharply aware of his other arm resting lightly against Rachel's as they lay side by side on the sand.

"We must both be crazy," Rachel said finally.

"Must be," he muttered.

"I was perfectly sane until I arrived on Kincaid Island. Correction . . . until you crawled into bed with me on Kincaid Island. It's been a nonstop roller-coaster ride ever since."

Rafe rolled onto his side and gently brushed some

sand from Rachel's cheek. "Feels like old times, doesn't it?"

She gave him a quick, desultory look, then shut her eyes, head tilted to the sun. "Too much so."

"You're tougher now, though," he said, his fingers finding themselves caught in strands of her hair.

"If I was so tough, I wouldn't keep letting myself get—" She didn't finish the sentence. "What do we do now?"

"What do you want to do?"

Rachel looked over at him again. "I was talking about getting back to the main island."

"Mmm-hmmm."

"Well . . . I should go check to see if there's a boat around."

"There's one in the shack behind the cottage," Rafe said idly.

Rachel glared at him, incensed. "Why didn't you—"

"It's got a half dozen holes in the bottom the size of walnuts. You might get as far as the sandbar in it before it sank."

"Maybe someone fixed it," she challenged, getting to her feet.

"Maybe." He sighed, stretching out more comfortably on the sand.

Rachel stomped off, only to return ten minutes later, her dress covered with dirt and grease, a smudged streak of sweat running down one cheek like war paint. She dropped on her knees to the sand.

"Make that two dozen holes . . . the size of saucers. Some little beaver's been busy out here."

He opened his eyes and looked up at her, laughing.

"Is it my wit or the way I look?" she asked dryly.

"A little of both."

"Somebody ought to clean out that shed one of these days. It looks like something out of a horror movie."

"Were you scared?" he said teasingly.

"I figured that, relatively speaking, I was safer in there than down here with you."

"You ought to take a swim and clean off," Rafe said blithely, following her gaze.

She hesitated. "I feel . . . awkward," she admitted falteringly, fully expecting a snappy comeback from Rafe. "There are no bathing suits back at the house."

Instead he gently caressed her back. "Go ahead, Rachel," he said softly. "If it will make you feel any better, I'll go take a dip around the other side of the cove."

"You will?"

"Scout's honor."

"You never were a scout."

He grinned. "Sit here arguing with me long enough and—"

"Okay, okay. I'll stop." She started to her feet, Rafe getting up first and helping her.

"Want me to unzip you?" he asked with a teasing smile.

"I want you to scram."

"Aye, aye, Captain. Just yell if you need me."

Ten minutes later that was exactly what she did.

Her voice pierced through the silence as she screamed his name out on the water. Rafe swam with strong, fierce strokes in her direction as she raced toward him at the same time.

"Oh, God, a shark. There's a shark in the water. I . . . saw it." She gasped, throwing her arms around Rafe's body and discovering that, like her, he had discarded all of his clothing for his swim.

"Take it easy, Rachel," he said soothingly. "There's never been a shark in these waters before."

"I don't care. Come on, hurry. We've got to get out of the water." She was still clutching him, too frightened to move despite her insistence to do so.

He pointed into the distance. "You mean that shark swimming out to sea?"

Rachel followed his finger. "Isn't it . . . a shark?"

"It looks like your garden-variety dolphin to me." His hands moved down to her spine, and he pressed her against him.

"Oh . . ."

But Rachel immediately forgot other threats, the potent threat of Rafe's naked body pressing against her own in the water the only thing on her mind. "I'm . . . sorry." Her fingers seemed to find their way into his wet hair of their own accord.

"I'd have to be a fool, as well as deaf, dumb, and blind, to say I was sorry," he murmured, his tongue licking the salty water beneath her earlobe.

His grip tightened, and though his hands were rough against her flesh, she felt only a bruising urgency. His tongue ran sinuously down the cord of her slender neck. Rachel could feel the shudder move through both their bodies.

When he abandoned his hold around her waist to cup her full, luscious breasts, Rachel trembled, having to cling to him now for strength. What an amazing sensation to feel hot fire course through her veins in the icy sea! She arched back as he lifted her so that he could capture first one nipple, then the other, in his hungry mouth, his tongue driving her wild as it alternately tugged and flicked over the tender buds with tantalizing skill.

She grabbed his hair tightly, wrenching his head toward hers, asking to be kissed. He needed no prodding. Instantly his mouth came over hers for a fevered kiss that demanded her complete acquiescence.

Rachel felt her body meld with Rafe's, her need for him matching his need for her. The fire had begun burning the moment they'd laid eyes on each other; now it was raging out of control. She kissed him back with a primitive urgency as he lifted her in his arms, carrying her to shore. Rachel felt drugged as she clung to him, holding tightly, feeling deliciously weightless, even as he finally fell with her onto the wet sand at the shoreline.

He kissed her again, a hard, slow, languorous kiss, then broke from her lips to trail a sensuous fire across her full breasts, then down along her rib cage and across her flat stomach.

He moved away just enough to gaze at her body, drinking it in with open hunger. His look alone was fiercely arousing to Rachel. She moaned, unable to quiet the animal lust that had so shockingly engulfed her.

"You're so incredibly beautiful," he whispered in a hot, sensual tone, his palm moving with a feathery lightness over her pink-tipped breasts. "More beautiful than before. More beautiful than a woman has a right to be."

Rachel smiled wantonly, her own eyes taking in Rafe's lean, muscled length. "Time hasn't changed some things. You've still got the same gorgeous body. So firm"—she let her fingers trail down his hard pectorals—"so golden"—then over his taut stomach—"so masculine."

He groaned as her fingers encircled him, caressing him with gentle strokes. The sensation that shot through him was unbelievable.

"You're so hot," she whispered.

"For you." His mouth nuzzled her throat, his tongue circling the pulsating hollow. Again he sought her straining nipple, his hands trailing under her buttocks as he moved on top of her.

Rachel's fingers glided over his warm, muscled flesh. She pressed her lips against his hair, her hips already thrusting in a slow, grinding motion against

94

him as she felt the insistent pressure of his need against her thigh.

Rafe could feel the flexing and straining of her firm buttocks. His hands slid lower, gripping her thighs, parting them as the throbbing intensity of his desire spiraled out of control. She cried out his name. And in that instant he took her.

Rachel felt him hot, hard, bursting inside of her. She cried out again, the sound no more than a ragged moan as a wild fire burned, quaking between her thighs as she met each thrust with a fury and hunger of her own.

They rolled in the wet sand, Rachel astride Rafe now, his hands gripping her waist tightly, arching her back, her creamy breasts thrust up proudly, her head tilted back, eyes closed, lips parted. Rafe could not imagine a more exquisite sight. He climaxed with her in a wild, frenzied fire storm of passion.

It was a long time before either of them could muster the energy to move. Rafe sat up, idly brushing off the sand from his chest, breathing in long gulps of air as he stared out to sea.

Rachel waited for Rafe to say something, although for the life of her she couldn't imagine what he would say. That he'd been right, no doubt. That it hadn't taken very much to get her to succumb. Succumb? That was a laugh. She'd done far more than submit to her ex-husband's seductive charms. She'd coaxed, urged, met his passion head-on. She was still in love with him. Now that was the real laugh. She was sure

Rafe Kincaid would get a great chuckle out of that tidbit of news.

But there was no sign of amusement in Rafe's face as he watched the rippling waves roll up to the shore, dancing around their feet. His closed expression hid the storm going on inside him. He was confounded by the swarm of confusing emotions tearing through him, as well as the sheer intensity of his feelings. Desire, anger, fear, wariness, all of these formed a spinning whirlpool in his mind. He'd thought he had it all figured out. He'd convinced himself that possessing Rachel this one time would quell the demons. He'd been wrong. Instead newer, far more powerful, demons had surfaced.

CHAPTER SIX

The silence was painful. Unable to bear it, Rachel got up and took long, running strides into the water. The splashing sound as she dived in had little effect on easing the tension caused by Rafe's sullen stillness. He didn't call to her or follow her. She didn't look back to shore as she swam with a fury. How ironic, she thought. She'd gone racing from one supposed shark right into the arms of another one. Rafe Kincaid was the last man on earth to run to for safety or security or protection—except of the most temporary kind.

Chilled and still miserable, Rachel turned back to shore. Rafe was gone. For a moment panic flooded her. But just as she started out of the water she saw him coming back from the direction of the cottage, dressed in his slacks and shirt and carrying a colorful beach towel. Now she wished that he had disappeared temporarily so that she could make it to shore with some semblance of dignity. Instead she was going to have to walk out of the sea stark naked, no doubt giving Rafe yet another amusing little lift.

She gritted her teeth, determined to show a modicum of class as she made her way to shore. She moved with a cool grace, taking the towel Rafe proffered. When he went to help drape it over her shoulders, she edged away, winding it sari-fashion around her slender frame.

Rafe regarded her with insolent indifference; Rachel was completely unaware that her own expression was calculated to appear equally removed. She scooped up her dress and walked silently up the path to the cottage.

They didn't say a word to each other back at the house, much less discuss their feelings about having made love. Rachel felt too confused and hurt by Rafe's reaction to be the one to bring it up, and it was clear that Rafe had no intention of sharing his feelings. On her way to the bathroom to shower, however, Rachel finally could endure the silence no longer.

"I hope either Ned or Liz know about this island and realize we're stranded. Otherwise we're likely to be stuck out here until Norah and Josh come out tomorrow." Rachel could hear how stiff her voice sounded as she waited for even the vaguest glimmer of tenderness to appear in Rafe's features. But as she stared at him, Rafe merely observed her with a quiet wariness.

"Why so glum, chum?" she demanded caustically. "You got what you wanted. You intended to break the rules all along. Well, at least we've settled that much." With that remark she stalked off to the bathroom and slammed the door. She took a quick, cold shower to wash the salt water off her body. When she stepped out, she heard Rafe calling to her from the other side of the locked door.

"Hurry up. The rescue party you were praying for has arrived," he said flatly.

Rachel dried off quickly, stepped into her silk panties, and slipped the yellow dress over her head.

She and Rafe were standing on the porch, silent foes, when a much agitated Ned Welles and an icy Liz Eastman came striding up the path.

"You two could have been stranded here all night if I hadn't spoken to Josh," Ned said, eyeing Rachel's new attire with a narrowed glance. "That wasn't particularly sporting of you to take off without me in the first place." He directed the last remark at Rafe, knowing full well that the little prank had been his doing.

"Maybe they didn't want your company," Liz said snidely.

Ned gave her a chilly stare.

Rachel got the strong feeling that while she and Rafe had been doing battle here, Liz and Ned had been involved in a battle of their own on Kincaid Island. She wondered if Liz had been fool enough to do more than battle. No, she decided, Liz wasn't a fool. Not as big a fool as she was.

"I was worried about you when you didn't come back from your walk," Ned said, directing this statement solely to Rachel. "Then I spoke to Josh and he mentioned the island. When I saw that one of the three sailboats was gone, I put two and two together."

"So how come you decided to play Boy Scout?" Rafe asked caustically.

Liz walked up the steps. "Actually, I was the one who panicked when I was out on one of the other sailboats and spotted yours—empty. I went back to the island and got Ned. I thought you really might have drowned." She smiled prettily. "It was a tremendous relief seeing you standing here on this porch." She put her hand on Rafe's arm and cast a dark look at Ned.

Rachel stiffened, only to feel Ned's hand reaching out for her arm. Without missing a beat she let him guide her down the steps and along the path ahead of Rafe and Liz. Rachel had a strong feeling that Ned and Liz were both caught up in the game of making each other jealous, but at this particular moment Rachel wasn't above playing along. She gave Ned a winsome smile.

"Are you all right?" Ned asked.

"I'm fine," she murmured absently, listening to the ripples of laughter, Liz's and Rafe's, behind her. She did not glance back to discover what was so amusing. Her face set in a tight grimace, she strode resolutely ahead.

Ned grinned. "You don't look like a woman who's had a particularly rewarding reunion with her ex-husband."

Rachel eyed him ruefully. "Oh, I was rewarded, all right. I got just what was coming to me."

No one talked much on the ride back to Kincaid

Island, although Liz seemed the most loquacious of the group. She had a habit of casually leaning against Rafe's shoulder whenever she spoke to him. And it didn't seem to phase her particularly that Rafe responded with a minimum of words.

Rachel, on the other hand, *was* phased by Rafe's actions—or lack of them. And what infuriated her the most was how undisturbed Rafe appeared to be. Oh, she knew his attention to Liz Eastman, however low-key it might be, was an intentional maneuver to put her rudely in her place. Still, he could have showed at least a glimmer of compassion for her distress. He'd set out to prove she still longed for him and he'd won. In victory he showed about as much grace as a sledge-hammer. To the winner the spoils. And to the loser?

Rachel went immediately to her room when they got back to the island, although Ned entreated her to sit out on the patio and have a drink with him. The three glasses of wine that she'd gulped at lunch, however, were doing enough of a number on her stomach. Besides, she had no desire to watch Liz Eastman flitter around Rafe solicitously for the rest of the afternoon.

The first thing she did when she got upstairs was to wrench the yellow sundress off, crumble it into a ball, and toss it in an empty bureau drawer. She'd tell Lois to take it away and burn it in the morning. So much for that reminder of the past. Too bad, she thought ruefully, she couldn't rid herself of Rafe so easily.

She felt a fierce desire to throw a nice, big, adolescent tantrum, her bottled-up rage at Rafe's indiffer-

101

ence desperately needing an outlet. But she held on to her composure. It was practically all she had left. Certainly she'd lost all claim to outrage and indignation. She'd asked for it . . . and she'd gotten it.

There was a rap on her door.

"Rachel?" Ned's voice was low.

She slipped on her flowered cotton robe. "Come in."

He opened the door with caution. "I didn't want to disturb you, but—"

She shrugged. "It doesn't matter. I'm plenty disturbed, anyway," she admitted.

He came inside and closed the door behind him. "Do you feel like talking about it?" He smiled. "I've been there myself."

"Liz?"

"I guess we're in the same boat, you and I. Maybe we can help each other."

Rachel put her palms to her temples. "My head's a little woozy, Ned. I'm not sure I follow any of what you're saying. If by 'the same boat' you mean that we're both suffering from unrequited love, you've got it wrong."

"Oh?"

"I don't love Rafe," she said with fierce bravado. "I don't even like him."

Ned sat down on the window seat, resting an elbow on his knee. He smiled broadly. "Now, how do you know that was what I thought we shared together? I certainly didn't say anything about still being in love with Liz."

102

Rachel did not hide her expression of disbelief, but Ned wasn't about to admit the truth of his feelings anymore than she was likely to admit the truth of hers.

She let out a weary sigh. "Well, what did you mean?"

He laughed softly. "I meant," he said, "that we're both up against two self-involved, overpowering individuals who are on full-blown ego trips. It's easy to get knocked over in their wake. I guess it isn't very macho of me to admit that Liz has a way of making me feel small at times. Women rarely have that kind of effect on me. No, wait. That sounds horribly chauvinistic."

Rachel arched a brow and nodded.

He grinned. "Let me amend that. People in general rarely make me feel inadequate. I'm not on an ego trip myself, but I usually feel pretty self-confident."

Rachel was sure of that.

"Anyway, I just thought it would be nice to feel we had each other, so to speak, when the going got a little rough." He stood up and walked over to her, placing a tentative hand on her cheek. "I find you very appealing, Rachel. There's a softness, a vulnerability about you that is even more tempting than your beauty. I like that in a woman."

Rachel flinched; she no more cared for Ned Welles's chauvinistic remarks than she did his calculated, if unstated, ploy to make his ex-fiancée jealous by coming on to her. She reached up to remove his hand from her face, but Ned completely misunderstood the gesture. Before Rachel realized what was happening, Ned's other hand immediately coiled around her, so that one of her arms was pinned against her side as his lips came down hard on her mouth.

Rachel was too astounded by Ned's abrupt assault to do anything at first. When she struggled with her free hand, Ned again misconstrued her intent, taking hold of her hand, drawing it around his neck, and holding it firm, so that she was now captured in a straitjacket grip that gave her absolutely no mobility. As she attempted to mumble a demand against his lips to be released, Ned used the opportunity to dart his tongue between her parted lips and deepen the kiss. A loud knock on the door startled them both. Rachel wrenched herself free just as Rafe opened the door.

He observed Ned coolly, then his eyes seemed to dwell on Rachel's face, especially, she felt, her lips— her just kissed lips. Or maybe it was the suddenly rosy hue in her complexion.

"Grand Central Station again," Rafe said with a dry smile. "Am I interrupting anything?"

Rachel, angry at herself for even caring that Rafe had almost walked in on her in the arms of another man, flared. "You are always interrupting as far as I'm concerned." She gave him a cool, haughty look. "Don't tell me this time there's a phone call for Mr. Welles?"

"The phone hasn't rung. You should know that, Rachel. I plugged your line in. Or"—he shot a quick, sardonic glance at Ned—"are you hearing bells, anyway?"

"What exactly is the reason for your appearance, Mr. Kincaid?" she asked acidly.

"I wanted to have a talk with you," he told her sharply.

"As far as I'm concerned, we have absolutely nothing to say to each other. Anyway, Ned and I were . . . having a discussion of our own before you so rudely walked in."

"I can't imagine, Kincaid, that you need much more of a brick to hit you to get Rachel's message," Ned said tautly.

"You know something, Welles, I didn't particularly care for you the moment I set eyes on you, but I couldn't really lay my finger on why." He shrugged laconically. "Well, I finally figured it out. You remind me of a vulture who swoops down for the kill while the body is still warm."

"Rafe," Rachel shrieked, "that's quite enough. How dare you!" She ran at him like a banshee, but this time Rafe was prepared. He caught her up in his arms and tossed her to Ned, who was less than five feet away from attempting to deck him one himself.

"Then again"—Rafe sneered at Rachel—"maybe I'm wrong about the body still being warm. You do seem to blow hot and cold these days with alarming regularity."

* * *

Dinner that night reminded Rachel of something out of a bad drawing-room drama. Dressed in formal attire, the whole group—she, Rafe, Liz, and Ned—behaved as if someone had rammed metal rods into their spines. The conversation consisted solely of "Please pass the salt" and "Please pass the pepper." Rachel imagined that any observer viewing the scene would have gotten more laughs out of it than a whole season's worth of *Sheer Madness.* However, none of the players, she possibly most of all, found a single thing even to smile about.

Even Liz Eastman, the woman Rachel would have voted the most effervescent of the group, remained curiously wooden throughout the meal. Rachel attributed that partly to Rafe's seeringly contemptuous manner. He was clearly not in the mood to be charming to anyone right at this moment. Instead he chose to don a belligerent sneer that Liz appeared to find too intimidating to attempt erasing.

Lois brought out dessert—slices of homemade banana cream pie.

"Can I get anyone anything else?" Lois asked, completely befuddled by the four sullen shakes of the head done nearly in unison. The atmosphere suggested an upcoming funeral rather than an upcoming wedding.

When dinner was over, Liz was the first to leave the table.

"I'm going to take a walk down by the beach," she announced, clearing her throat. As she spoke, her glance skidded past Ned and Rachel, lingering for a dramatic moment on Rafe. He didn't, however, appear to take notice, although Rachel observed that Ned made surreptitious note of Liz's gaze. She also observed the flicker of jealousy that flashed in his eyes as Liz exited.

Ned stood up next, moving to the back of Rachel's chair. His hands rested lightly on her shoulders. "Shall we go into the library for an after-dinner drink?" Ned was turning out to be the best actor of the ensemble.

As she was about to decline, not feeling any more desire to fend off Ned's maneuvers than she did her ex-husband's, she caught Rafe's insolent smile and immediately changed her mind. "That sounds like a good idea," she said with a curt nod.

"Great idea," Rafe concurred, rising at the same moment Rachel stood. She glared at him across the table, but Rafe merely smiled charmingly. Rachel decided she preferred the sneering contemptuousness. At least that was real.

It was Rafe who led the way to the library. After all, although Ned had been a far more frequent visitor to the island these past few years since joining up with Josh in business, it was still Rafe's home. And so it was Rafe, too, who did the honors of serving the cognacs. Then he stood regally at the ornate marble mantle, the model of the perfect country gentleman. But even in his elegantly cut dinner jacket, there was no hiding the look of the rugged adventurer that was as much a part of him as the air he breathed. There was nothing, when it came down to it, that could ever detract from Rafe Kincaid's raw masculinity.

"Tell me a little about your work, Rachel," Ned said, breaking the tense silence. "It must be very exciting to be part of a successful TV show."

"Do you watch *Sheer Madness,* Welles?" Rafe asked with a benign smile.

"Actually . . . I haven't." Ned said, keeping his voice civil. He was determined not to succumb to Rafe Kincaid's gibes. "But I certainly will now that I know the associate producer of the show personally."

Rafe didn't miss the seductive smile Ned gave Rachel. "I would have thought you went in for more erudite, sophisticated stuff," he said with a snicker.

Rachel wasn't sure if, by "stuff," Rafe was referring to the show or to her, but she gave him an insolent look that covered either possibility.

Ned walked over and stood beside Rachel. "You're wrong, Kincaid. I think a touch of 'sheer madness' can be quite exhilarating." He winked at Rachel.

But Rachel was not in the mood to indulge either Ned or Rafe in their adolescent behavior, and she abruptly set her untouched cognac down and strode across the room to the French doors leading outside. "I think I could use a little air myself," she announced coolly. "And no," she added before either man could say a word, "I do not want company."

When she got closer to the beach, Rachel's pace slowed. Liz Eastman was out here somewhere, and

Rachel really wasn't in the mood to run into her. What she needed . . . Lord, she had no idea what she needed. No, that wasn't true, either. She still needed Rafe. That was what was driving her crazy. She could not relinquish the memory of the ecstasy she had felt, the ecstasy they both had shared when they'd made love today, even though he'd been so cold and unfeeling afterward. It hurt terribly that he seemed to treat their moment of abandon as though it never happened.

She continued walking slowly toward the beach, as there was no sign of Liz. Then, just before she got to a cluster of scrub pine, she heard a soft whimpering sound. It sounded like a bird, but a moment later Rachel picked up a distinctly feminine sniffle. Rachel's first impulse was to hurry along. She had more than enough of her own grief to handle. But she couldn't just rush off.

She called Liz's name from a safe enough distance so that the woman could pull herself together or simply remain silent so that Rachel would get the message that she didn't want to be disturbed, a sentiment Rachel would understand readily.

Instead the sniffling turned into a resounding sob. A few moments later Rachel found Liz Eastman, usually a picture of elegance, sophistication, and sublime arrogance, sitting in a most ignoble heap on the cold, damp earth.

Rachel immediately thought Liz had fallen and injured herself. She rushed to her aid, only to stumble over a fallen tree limb and go plummeting headfirst to the ground, feeling a sharp pain shoot up her leg. Lately she seemed to be having a great deal of trouble keeping her feet safely planted beneath her.

Her surprising entrance abruptly cut off Liz's sobs. "Rachel, are you all right?" she said between little breathy shudders.

Rachel got to a sitting position. "I'm not sure. What about you?"

"Me? Oh, I'm just fine and dandy," she said in a silly falsetto voice that made Rachel smile.

"No, you're not. You're miserable. Believe me, I recognize misery when I see it. I'm experienced in those matters."

Liz sniffled loudly. "He is a bastard," she muttered.

Rachel couldn't argue there.

"He is absolutely the most smug, supercilious, arrogant man I've ever run across."

"You won't hear any argument from me on any of those accounts," Rachel said firmly, feeling suddenly that she and Liz at least shared one thing in common: their assessment of Rafe Kincaid.

"I don't know how you can tolerate his absolutely blatant disrespect. I'm telling you, Rachel, I've worked too hard and too long to be put in my place by some—"

"Smug, supercilious, arrogant bastard?" Rachel helped her out.

"Exactly." Liz lifted the hem of her strapless chiffon dress and wiped her mascara-coated eyes.

110

"Exactly," Rachel said, concurring.

"Well, let me tell you something, Rachel . . . you're welcome to him. I couldn't care less."

Rachel gave Liz a sidelong glance. "I don't want him. However," she said archly, "I really don't think it's your place to offer him."

"Huh?" Liz muttered, scratching her arm vigorously. "God, do you suppose I've brushed against some poison ivy? I'm highly allergic. I barely have to look at the stuff and . . ." She sighed wearily, getting to her feet. "That's all I need. That would be the final straw to this fiasco. I swear, you never really know a man until after you break up with him. Let me give you a word of advice, Rachel. If you have any sense of dignity or pride, don't lower yourself to playing the helpless damsel in distress for Ned. Oh, he'll eat it up. He adores spouting his chauvinistic—"

"Wait a second," Rachel said, taking hold of Liz's skirt. "Who was it you were talking about this whole time? Rafe or Ned?"

"Rafe?" Liz's tone was astounded. "Why, I don't find Rafe the least bit chauvinistic. He's a bit moody, but that's to be expected. Any man who constantly confronts peril, risking his life in the four corners of the globe for those fantastic photos, is allowed to have his moods. Frankly, Rachel, I don't know what you see in Ned."

A small smile curved Rachel's lips. "Don't you?"

"Absolutely not," she protested quickly. Too quickly, in Rachel's estimation. It didn't take a mind

111

reader to know that Liz was still in love with Ned. Her fervent protest alone, not to mention her stinging jealousy, was proof enough.

"Anyway," Liz said, hastening to go on, "I thought, at first, you might still be carrying a torch for Rafe."

"Oh, I'm carrying a torch, all right." Rachel sneered. "Only I want to bounce it right off his head." She went to stand up, only to fall back to the ground with a sharp cry. "My calf . . ." She winced. "I have a cramp in my muscle. It must have happened when I tripped over the log before."

"Here, let me help you," Liz said, stretching out a hand. "I just hope you aren't as allergic to poison ivy as I am. I'm beginning to itch all over."

Rachel discovered that she couldn't put even the slightest pressure on her right foot. She sat back down and gave Liz a wry smile. "I don't suppose you could give me a piggyback ride?"

"I'd better go get . . . Ned to carry you back."

Rachel sighed wearily. "I guess you'll have to. Do me a favor, though, Liz. I'd just as soon not have Rafe know about my . . . little difficulty. Try to get Ned off alone before you tell him what happened."

Liz hesitated.

"Is there a problem?" Rachel asked.

"It's just . . . well, will you answer a question, Rachel?"

"What is it?"

"Are you really attracted to Ned?"

"I honestly don't know why you think . . ."

"He apparently thinks you're a very warm, responsive woman."

Rachel gave Liz a sympathetic smile. "I'm not attracted to Ned. And he's not really attracted to me, either. Don't you see what he's doing? He's trying to make you rip-roaring jealous by playing up to me. And from where I'm standing"—she grinned—"sitting, I mean, he's doing a damn good job of it."

Liz pulled back her shoulders indignantly. "He's doing no such thing. I still can't believe I was actually fool enough, once upon a time, to have even considered marrying the man."

Rachel looked bleakly up at Liz's departing figure, wondering what kind of fool that made her. A bigger one than Liz, obviously.

When she heard footsteps less than two minutes later, Rachel was puzzled. Even if Liz *ran* back to the house, an unlikely possibility, it would take a good five minutes, not to mention the additional five it would take for Ned to come fetch her.

"I'm over here," she called out cautiously when the footsteps drew closer.

She looked up sharply as Rafe appeared out of the shadows.

"What are you doing here?" she asked. The trembling in her voice unnerved her almost as much as seeing Rafe standing there looking down at her.

"I ran into Liz as I was walking to the beach. She said you hurt your leg." He gave Rachel a puzzled look. "Did you ask her not to tell me?"

113

"Why would I do that?"

"She acted so skittish about it."

He knelt down beside her. "Can you walk on it at all?"

"Would I be sitting here on the wet ground if I could?" she snapped.

"Temper, temper. You always did get mad whenever you were sick."

"How would you know? You were rarely around when I was suffering."

"What about that time you came down with the flu when we were in Saudi Arabia?"

"It served me right for ever agreeing to join you on that assignment," she said irritably.

"I missed two days in the field trying to play Florence Nightingale, but all you did was sulk and refuse to be pampered."

"Actually, I like being pampered. Not all the time, but I happen to appreciate a little attention when I'm sick."

"You could have fooled me."

"Ah, but you didn't fool me one bit. You resented giving up those two days. Oh, you acted the part of Florence Nightingale as far as your behavior was concerned, but you never put any . . . heart behind it. If you remember, that was the last assignment I ever agreed to join you on."

Rafe avoided her angry stare and lifted her leg gently to survey the damage. There was a full moon out and plenty of stars, so he was able to see fairly well.

"It's just a muscle cramp," she said, unable to mask the hint of breathlessness in her voice. "It hurts like crazy now, but it should work itself out in a few hours." Rachel felt a rush of tormented arousal at his bare touch on her skin. She wanted to recoil, but she was in too much pain to do anything but submit to his examination.

He finally released her. "I'll have to carry you back."

Seeing that she had no other choice, she gave a chilly nod of her head. However, when he lifted her in his strong, capable arms, her iciness melted, scorched by Rafe's own rising heat.

He made no attempt to move for a moment, his piercing blue eyes holding hers. "Was I really all that bad, Rachel?"

She dropped the facade for an instant. "I guess neither one of us was all that good at marriage," she said sadly. "Like you said, we were both moving in the direction of that fork in the road all along."

Rafe's expression turned sardonic. "Right. Only I guess I didn't realize at the time that you were moving at such a fast speed."

CHAPTER SEVEN

Rafe carried Rachel back into the house. As they passed the library they could hear Ned and Liz in a heated discussion. Walking swiftly by, Rafe took Rachel directly up to her room and set her down on her bed. Then, without a word, he turned and left. Rachel fully expected him not to return, but a few minutes later he reappeared with a tube of liniment. He shrugged off his dinner jacket and carelessly unfastened his bow tie, after which he undid the first few buttons of his shirt. Then he sat down on the bed and reached for her leg.

"I can manage myself," she said coolly, trying to avoid his very masculine chest.

Rafe merely scowled, his large, strong hand easily reaching around her ankle.

Rachel winced as he gently but firmly applied the liniment to the sore area at the back of her calf. "What were you doing in the brush, anyway?" he muttered. "I thought you were going down to the beach."

"What difference does it make?" she said sullenly, trying to wrench her leg free. But Rafe's grip was too strong. "That hurts," she snapped.

"I guess I never will get the angel of mercy bit down well enough," he said, smiling grimly.

Rachel let out a small sigh of relief as he stopped massaging the greasy ointment into her leg to squeeze some more out of the tube. Rachel grabbed for it at the same time. "I'm perfectly capable . . ."

"I know all about your perfect capabilities," he said, cutting her off, then grabbing her wrist and extracting the tube from her grasp. "Now, I may not be Florence Nightingale, but I have picked up a bit of first aid in the field. Just shut up and let me get on with it," he said tautly, pushing her flat down on the bed.

As she fell back her dress rode up, revealing more of her long, shapely legs. Rafe felt a surge of pure desire as he looked down at her. A few hours ago those slender legs had been wrapped around him, pressing against his naked flesh, urging him on. . . .

Rachel propped herself on her elbows, and Rafe abruptly pulled her dress back down, quickly finishing with the massage. He could feel Rachel's eyes watching him steadily.

"How does that feel?" he asked brusquely.

"Fine." Her own tone matched his.

He looked up at her. She looked away.

"Well . . . I guess that should do it, then." He hesitated. "Do you need some help getting undressed?"

"No," she said so quickly that Rafe had to smile.

"I don't believe in taking advantage of a woman when she's down," he quipped.

Rachel arched a brow. "Really? I thought that was how you preferred your women."

Rafe grinned. "You've got a stinging tongue, Rachel."

"It comes with experience," she replied tartly.

"Tell me, do you whiplash Ned Welles in a similar fashion?"

"Ned Welles? I hardly know him. I usually require a round or two before I warm up."

"I thought I walked in on round one. When I interrupted you and Ned having your . . . discussion."

"I don't see that what Ned and I discuss is any of your business."

Rafe shrugged. "I just don't want to see you getting hurt."

Rachel let out a haughty laugh. "And I accused you of not being solicitous. Tell me something, Rafe. Since I'd hate to see you getting hurt as well, don't you think you ought to show a touch of restraint around Liz Eastman? I mean, I got the feeling that you have . . . an ongoing relationship with that woman—your assistant, the adept photojournalist whom you trust so much. Doesn't she expect to be able to trust you as well?"

Rafe's shrewd eyes held her in a steady gaze. "Then what do you suppose she'd think about the fact that I made passionate love to my ex-wife today? And enjoyed every moment of it."

Rachel halted, stiffening instantly. "You . . .

didn't appear to be so happy about it," she said, faltering.

"We broke our rule," he said in a low voice.

"Since when does breaking a rule phase Rafe Kincaid?"

"Since I realized that making love to you again holds many more dangers than I feel ready to handle."

Rachel's heart was pounding as she looked into Rafe's almost ruthless eyes, unable to acknowledge the glimmer of sad regret she saw there as well. "Pity you didn't think about that before. . . ."

The muscles along Rafe's jaw were tautly flexed. "There are some things you only learn the hard way." He stood up, took a quick look at her leg, and, in five long strides, was out the door.

By the next morning the cramp had all but gone in Rachel's calf. But while her physical condition had improved, her mood hadn't. Why was it that every time she and Rafe had any kind of exchange at all, she always felt afterward that it had been left unfinished? The number of unfinished fragments was accumulating faster than Rachel could keep track of. Her nerves were frayed, and she could not shake the rage inside of her that constantly threatened to boil over.

When she arrived in the breakfast room, she found Ned sitting alone at the table. He glanced up as she entered, but he looked distracted.

For a moment Rachel put aside her own grief as she sat down across from Ned and observed his grim expression.

"Is something wrong?" she asked.

"What? No." He seemed to pull himself together as she poured some coffee into his empty cup. His expression abruptly turned solicitous. "What about you? How's your leg?"

"I'll live," she said with a wry smile. "For it all, I am a survivor." She poured herself a cup of coffee. "Where's Liz this morning? Already working?"

"She's . . . indisposed," he said sullenly.

"Oh."

"Poison ivy."

"Oh," she said with more understanding. "Is it bad?"

Ned stared into his coffee. "Rafe is attending to her."

"Oh." She mimicked Ned's downcast stare.

There was a long silence.

"Do you see what I mean?" Ned commented suddenly.

"No," Rachel admitted. "Mean about what?"

"About Rafe being on a full-blown ego trip." Ned lifted his head, his eyes level with hers. "Your ex-husband certainly likes to cover all bases. You . . . Liz. I imagine that if the housekeeper were twenty years younger, he would have made a play for her as well. No wonder you divorced him."

Rachel bristled. "Rafe was never unfaithful to me when we were married."

"Really?" He cocked his head, a rueful glint in his eye. "How can you be so sure? From what Josh has

120

told me, Rafe spent most of your marriage on assignments all over the world."

"And I happened to have gone with him on many of them," she said tartly.

"But not all." He said suggestively.

Rachel's narrowed gaze sliced across at him. "You barely know Rafe Kincaid. You certainly have no right whatsoever to disparage his character or his . . . morals. Anyway, Mr. Welles, why don't we focus on the present? Something tells me you are just as interested as my ex-husband in covering all bases."

A ribbon of red began to rise in Ned's neck above the collar of the white Lacoste polo jersey he was wearing. "I have no idea what that remark is supposed to mean."

"It's supposed to mean," she said evenly, "that you're still in love with Liz Eastman and yet you have absolutely no qualms about making persistent passes at me."

"You don't say," he said in a clipped, affected tone. The redness was now creeping up over his jaw, and he was blinking fiercely. "If we are going to talk about having no qualms, Miss Mason, I suggest you look in your own backyard."

"What the hell is that supposed to mean?"

"It means," he said tightly, "that you apparently have no qualms about throwing yourself at Rafe and at me with barely a second to catch your breath in between."

"Why you . . . ?" Impelled by her fury, Rachel

121

leapt up, leaned across the table, and thrust out her arm, her fist connecting with his jaw.

Fortunately for Ned her punch lacked a wallop, as she'd been forced to stretch across a fairly wide table in order to land her blow. Still, he was taken aback by the assault and stared at her with dazed eyes, mindlessly rubbing his jaw.

Rachel muttered something before she turned around to leave, but Ned couldn't be sure if it was an apology or a colorful expletive.

She hesitated for a moment as she saw Rafe standing in the doorway. It was obvious from the amused expression on his face that he'd witnessed at least the finale to her exchange with Ned. Tilting her chin, she started out of the room.

"Lovely day, isn't it?" Rafe commented idly as she passed him.

"Shut up," she said acidly, hearing Rafe's low chuckle as she strode into the hall.

Liz was at the top of the stairs, her arms and legs covered in what looked like salmon-colored paint but which Rachel surmised to be calamine lotion. As Rachel headed up toward her she saw that Liz's face, while free of poison ivy, held a pinched expression.

"I guess you were right last night," Rachel said. "About the poison ivy . . . and especially about Ned Welles."

Liz's green eyes held a hard sheen. "The only thing I was wrong about was your ex-husband," Liz said haughtily. "He's the moodiest man I've ever come across. He barely treated me civilly this morning. You'd think he had the weight of the world sitting right on his shoulders. He was so charming yesterday, and this morning he's as surly and sour as a lemon. I swear; men—who needs them?" Irate, Liz wheeled around and headed back to her room. Seconds later Rachel heard a door slam loudly.

Rachel was certain Liz's ill humor was due to more than the sullen mood of a man she hardly knew. The tension was fast escalating between the warring factions. A weary sigh crossed Rachel's lips. "Who needs them, indeed?"

She was about to continue up the stairs when the front door opened. Rachel peered down to see her sister, Norah, enter the front hall.

Rachel turned and came down the stairs. "At last. A touch of sanity . . ." She swallowed the rest of her words as she saw the grim look on her sister's face. "What is it, Norah? What's wrong? Has something happened to—"

"It's off," Norah broke in. She stared past Rachel. "The wedding is off."

Norah's loud declaration drew both Ned Welles and Rafe into the hall. Rachel glanced over at them, shrugging her shoulders in bafflement.

"Norah . . ." Rachel said gently. "Come upstairs and we'll talk about it in private."

Norah shook her head violently, hot tears streaking her face. "I don't want to talk about it. I just want

123

. . . to be left . . . alone." Racing past Rachel, then Ned and Rafe, Norah tore up the stairs.

For the second time Rachel heard the loud slam of a bedroom door.

"What do you think that was all about?" Ned said in amazement.

"I don't have any idea," Rachel said, staring dumbfoundedly up at the stairs. "I'll go up and try to talk to her."

"No," Rafe said firmly. "Let me try."

Rachel looked leery. "Rafe, I don't think—"

"What's going on?" Liz asked, coming down the stairs. "I heard the commotion down here and then, when I was stepping out of my room, I saw Norah fly by me, sobbing."

"She's calling off the wedding," Ned told her.

Liz came up to Rachel. "Why? What happened?"

"I haven't the foggiest idea," Rachel muttered as she saw Rafe take the steps two at a time. Maybe he could get through to Norah. She certainly hadn't had much luck.

The latest shocker of the day made matters inestimably more tense. Armed camp, indeed, Rachel thought. Kincaid Island was becoming a regular war zone.

The last warrior arrived an hour later. Rachel was tensely pacing across the thick Oriental carpet in the library, waiting for Rafe or Norah to reappear and fill her in on what was happening when Josh Kincaid burst into the room like a man possessed.

"Where is she?"

Rachel stared openmouthed at Josh. In all the years she had known him she'd rarely seen a single brown hair out of place. Now his hair was tousled, his blue suit disheveled; even his shirttail was dangling out from his waistband. And as he came closer she observed that he reeked of whiskey. Josh rarely imbibed, but he'd apparently made up for lost time.

"Rachel, don't stand there gaping. She is here, isn't she?"

Rachel nodded. "She's upstairs." Gathering her wits, she added, "Rafe's up there trying to talk to her. He must be doing okay. It's been an hour."

Josh hesitated, then he walked over to the bar and poured himself a stiff whiskey. He downed it in one long swallow. He immediately poured himself another.

"What happened, Josh?"

"You tell me, Rachel." He sat down wearily on the couch, cupping his drink in both hands. "We were having a discussion about the wedding last night . . . and somehow we got to talking about you and Rafe." He gave Rachel a wan look. "It was such a dumb argument, really. We started discussing what went wrong with your marriage and ended up fighting about all the things likely to go wrong with ours."

Rachel stiffened, but Josh didn't notice. He laughed dryly, then finished off the second drink. "We covered every possible catastrophe. I told Norah she was a lot like Rafe, wanting to dash off to Paris and God knows where after that. She apparently feels that staying home and concentrating on our marriage is simply not exciting enough for her. Norah, in turn, decided I was just like you, Rachel, always needing to be in control, feeling this irrational need to be tied . . . no . . . she used the word *shackled*. Yes, 'shackled to tradition' was how she put it."

"Shackled to tradition, am I?" Rachel muttered with a scowl.

Josh seemed not to hear her or else was too caught up in his own anger to respond. He stood up and walked to the bar to pour himself another drink. Rachel frowned. "Don't you think you ought to go easy on that stuff, Josh? It has a way of creeping up on you."

Josh merely shrugged. "Norah kept saying how she could identify with Rafe, how she wasn't so sure she liked the idea of being dictated to any more than he did. Dictated to? I didn't know what she was talking about. All of a sudden she went on this spiel about being stifled, needing her freedom, and accusing me of wanting to keep her safely under my thumb. She claimed she was the one making all the compromises in our relationship." His features hardened. "I never asked Norah to give up anything for me. I simply asked her to marry me. We can't very well have much of a marriage if she's off for two years on some damn research project." His fists clenched tightly. "I swear, I don't know what's gotten into her all of a sudden."

"I think it's called premarital panic. It hits all us brides," Rachel said gently, placing her hand on Josh's

126

shoulder. "She'll come around. Just give her a little while to work the jitters out." Rachel tried to sound confident, but she was growing more alarmed at the idea that Norah was conferring with exactly the wrong role model up in her room. Rafe, no doubt, was supporting every one of her statements about needing to feel free, hating to be tied down, going after what she wanted.

"I don't know, Rachel," Josh was saying meanwhile. "Maybe we are doing the wrong thing. It isn't that I don't have my own . . . concerns about getting married. There are times I wake up in the middle of the night in a sweat, afraid that I'm making more of a commitment than I can handle. I've been a bachelor for a long time."

"Josh, look me straight in the eye and tell me you're not in love with Norah," Rachel demanded.

Josh met her gaze a bit blearily, but there was a cool reserve in his eyes. "I would think you'd be the first to admit that love alone doesn't insure success in a marriage."

Rachel compressed her lips. She was saved from having to somehow convince Josh that her personal marital failure had no connection to his and Norah's chances by Rafe's arrival in the library.

Josh looked up sharply.

"She took a tranquilizer," Rafe said, walking over to his brother. "You look like you could use one yourself."

"He's already had several glasses of whiskey since

he arrived—and who knows what he guzzled before he got here," Rachel pointed out.

Rafe took the glass from Josh's hands. "Why don't you get some rest?"

Josh, drifting into a semi-stupor from the liquor and from not having slept in the last twenty-four hours, nodded slowly. But when Rafe helped him to his feet, he suddenly jerked away. "What the hell did she say?" he said, erupting.

Rafe sighed. "She says she doesn't want to get married." He saw the fury rise in his brother's face. "Take it easy, Josh. Don't jump to conclusions."

"Don't jump to conclusions?" he bellowed, swaying precariously on his feet. "She's called off the wedding. What other conclusion is there to . . . to conclude?" His words grew increasingly slurred.

Rafe caught him by the shoulders. "She loves you, damn it. And she's scared. If you go flying off the handle now, you're going to blow it."

"I'm not . . . flying off the . . . handle," he muttered, falling against Rafe. "Will you stand still . . . while I'm talking . . . to you?"

Rafe and Rachel exchanged a smile. "Come on. I'll help you up to your room and you can sack out for a couple of hours."

Josh tilted his head back as if suddenly realizing that he was seeing his brother for the first time in fourteen months. "Rafe. How the hell are you, Rafe?" He leaned over conspiratorially. "Rachel's here, you know. I hope . . . it's gonna be okay?" He went to give Rafe a friendly punch in the shoulder but missed the target, swiping the air instead. "She's a great gal, Rafe."

"Yeah, Josh, I know." He glanced at Rachel, but she had trouble meeting his gaze.

"And . . . she's beautiful, Rafe. I mean, the woman . . . is beautiful," Josh muttered as he allowed his brother to half carry him toward the door.

Rafe grinned. "She's beautiful, all right."

"Right," Josh agreed. At the door he came to a sudden halt. "Wait a sec . . . who are we talking about?"

"Come on, Josh."

"Take Norah now." He gripped Rafe's arm. "She's not exactly . . . beautiful, but . . . there's something about her. You know what I mean, Rafe. There's really something . . . about her that . . . just . . . drives me crazy." With that Josh's head rolled back and his body went entirely limp.

Rachel helped Rafe drag Josh upstairs. As they passed Norah's door Rafe stopped. He glanced at the door, then at Josh, slumped against him in a stupor, and then at Rachel, a devilish glint in his eye.

Rachel tilted her head. "You aren't thinking what I think you're thinking, are you?"

"I think it's a great idea. Why, they'll probably wake up in each other's arms in a few hours and they won't even remember what the hell they were fighting about."

"Rafe . . . it's a dirty trick to play on them."

He grinned. "But we both love pulling stunts, don't we?"

Rachel started to protest, but then her own dark blue eyes sparkled. "Well, it might work. If it did, we'll have done them the biggest favor of their lives." She hesitated. "I hope."

"Get the door and see if she's asleep," Rafe commanded, taking full charge of Josh.

Rachel opened the door and softly called Norah's name as she saw her sister stretched out on the bed. When there was no answer, she helped Rafe drag Josh inside.

A few minutes later Rachel leaned against the wall in the corridor to catch her breath. "Norah may never forgive me for this one."

Rafe leaned beside her. "I'll take the blame. I'll tell them it was strictly my doing." He captured her hand. "Let's go take some food down to the beach and have a breakfast picnic." He cast her a teasing smile. "I noticed that you didn't get a chance to eat before."

Rachel started to frown, but suddenly she burst into laughter. "Ned never saw my knuckle sandwich coming." She giggled. "But he deserved it."

Rafe laughed with her, pulling his arm around her. "I would have paid a million bucks to see that look of sheer shock on his face."

Rachel leaned into him, laughing harder. "I swear, I think the whole batch of us must be mad." All at once she became acutely aware of the feel of Rafe's strong, hard body as he pressed her more tightly to him.

"I know I'm mad, Rachel," he murmured against her hair.

"Rafe . . . please."

"Let's postpone the picnic for a couple of hours," he murmured, close to her ear.

She tried to twist free. "Rafe, this is crazy. You can't stand here trying to seduce me in the middle of the hallway."

"You're right."

"Rafe . . . I don't like that glint in your eye," she said in warning as he took her hand and started leading her down the hall.

"You did ask me to seduce you in a more private place?"

"I did . . . no such thing."

They were at his door. He turned the knob. But Rachel stood firm. "You must think I'm a complete fool."

"No. I don't think you're a fool, Rachel."

"We've gone this route already, and it didn't get us anywhere."

He moved very, very close to her without any part of them touching. "I thought we got clear up to heaven yesterday." His voice was smooth as velvet, as searing as a fiery inferno.

"Rafe, don't do this to me," she pleaded, unable to look away from his eyes, as though they held her with a strange magnetic force. "I wasn't talking about yesterday." She could hardly get her lips to stop quivering. "I was talking about five years ago."

"Tell me about yesterday, Rachel. It was good for you, wasn't it? You still want me. I know you do. Why don't we stop fighting it?"

She felt immobilized as he leaned a fraction closer, his lips brushing hers. Then his arm was around her, not demanding a response this time. Rachel knew he was waiting for her to make up her own mind. He wasn't going to coerce her—just give her some very friendly persuasion.

"What about the dangers?" she whispered, riddled with confusion, desire and fear overwhelming her. If she could pull back now, she knew it would save her endless grief and self-reproach later. But Rafe was so compelling, so wildly erotic. She was so in love with him. He brought her to a place that was all their own. He made her soar. He made her forget reason, inhibition.

His lips met hers again, his tongue scorching her with longing as it swept across her mouth. "Maybe," he whispered, kissing her harder, "we just have to live dangerously."

As he went to pull his head back Rachel's arms moved around his neck. "I am crazy, Rafe. I am. I am," she repeated over and over as her lips moved along his craggy jaw; his dark-lashed, mesmerizing eyes; his hungry, eager, intoxicating mouth. "I am—so damn crazy—about you."

When he swept her in his arms and drew her into the room, Rachel held on to him for dear life, knowing only that for better or for worse, she still belonged to Rafe Kincaid.

CHAPTER EIGHT

Rafe framed her face in his hands. "Slow down, baby."

Rachel knew that anxiety as much as desire was making her want to race pell-mell into lovemaking. She didn't want to think. Only feel. She was terrified that at any moment an inner voice would scream at her to stop. And she didn't want to stop. She felt possessed. She wanted to be possessed. Only Rafe didn't want just sex; he wanted her to make love *with* him. He was insisting that she be there with him emotionally as well as physically.

His fingers slowly undid the top three buttons on her blouse, letting his fingertips languidly trail along the revealed vee of silken flesh. He lifted her chin. "Smile for me, Rachel." He kissed her lips lightly. "Just like that first time. Oh God, Rachel . . . what a time that was. I had no idea I was your first lover. I'd never met a woman who was at once so utterly sexual and so unbelievably innocent." As he spoke in soft whispers he began undressing her.

His hands stroked and caressed her as he peeled off each garment, and Rachel could feel the muscles in her body start to relax. She even smiled. "I was terrible that first time. I wanted so desperately to please you. I wanted . . . it to be so good for you."

Rafe's hands slid up her rib cage and cupped her breasts. "Oh Rach . . ." he murmured, pressing his mouth ever so gently against one sweet, taut nipple, "don't you know how incredible that first time was for me? I felt as if"—he looked into her eyes—"as if I had discovered the secret of the universe. It was the purest, most perfect moment I'd ever known."

Rachel stared spellbound at Rafe, astonished to see real tears in his eyes. Such an extraordinary sight. She had never seen him show such a telling sign of vulnerability. It made her whole body tremble. Not once during their courtship or their marriage did she experience this intense feeling of connectedness with Rafe. He touched her more deeply than she'd ever imagined possible, because for the first time, even if it never was to happen again, he made her see how deeply she had touched him.

She reached out her hand, her fingers delicately caressing the corner of his eye. Then he captured her wrist, pressing her palm against his mouth.

He kissed her fiercely then, a long, drugging kiss. Rachel drank in the taste of him, pulling off his shirt in her eagerness to feel his warm, masculine body against hers. This time Rafe didn't entreat her to slow down. She could feel him growing hard against her thigh. She opened her eyes as they continued kissing. So did Rafe. There were no tears there now, only fierce, hot desire, the same desire he saw reflected in her eyes.

They fell together onto the bed, laughing as they realized that in her job of stripping him she'd forgotten his socks. She slithered down his body, her mouth and her hands taking sublime pleasure in caressing, exploring, tempting every inch of his flesh. As her lips skimmed his inner thigh Rafe let out a ragged moan. Even the way she removed his socks, letting her fingers lightly trail the arches of his feet, drove him crazy.

Rachel thrilled to the excitement she brought him. It made her feel light-headed, daring, wanton. Every touch, every stroke, every movement was fluid, mystifying, delicious. She had never felt so self-possessed. Her lips brushed across his rock-hard abdomen, then lower, lingering, absorbing Rafe's fierce response.

Rafe's hands stroked her hair, her neck, her shoulders. His touch was like fire, urging her on. Her lips parted, and she drew him into her mouth greedily, recklessly.

"Oh, Rach . . ." he whispered huskily, feeling her incredible, wild heartbeat pounding against his thigh as her mouth, her lips, her tongue wreaked havoc on his body and his mind. She stirred him as no other woman ever had. To be lost within himself was a rare sensation for Rafe, but this lovemaking with Rachel electrified him, removed him completely from his own fears, even his own performance. For once in his life he didn't have to take complete charge. He wasn't forced to guide Rachel, to encourage her, to teach her. It was as if she knew his body far better than he himself did. And that she knew his soul . . .

Later . . . later there would be a resurrection of that list of dangers. Later he would remind himself that he lived in an impermanent, ephemeral world, and he would remember that distancing had always been his stock-in-trade, his safety valve, his escape route. But now, with Rachel, he let himself feel the bonding, the closeness, the sheer need. The love.

He lifted her finally, rolling her over onto her back, kissing her at the same time, deep, tongue-plunging kisses that took her breath away. Their desire was soaring now, Rachel feeling free, unbound by any restrictions, physically and mentally. She loved him, she wanted him, there was nothing else in the world that ever felt so right to her. Her palms massaged him, thrilling to the play of muscles along his back. As he entered her she was aware of herself and Rafe only, all sense of time and place lost, her body rushing with the wind.

She gave herself up completely to sensation, her body transmitting the ecstasy like rippling waves of the sea, feeling them endless, eternal. They climaxed together with a cry that seemed to echo in the room.

Afterward they laughed softly as they felt their diaphragms expand and contract heavily against each other's chests. He held her tightly, a bear hug, his mouth nuzzling her neck. She squirmed in his arms as he darted his tongue across her skin.

"That tickles." She giggled.

"A good tickle or a bad tickle?" he whispered against her skin.

"Mmmm. A good tickle." She sighed, finding it absolutely incredible to feel aroused again after so short a time. She pressed her hips against him. "Mmmm. Good for you too."

He laughed again, then his voice was tender. "So good. So very good, Rachel." He edged back her thick, dark hair that shadowed half her face.

Rachel ran her fingertips over the hard outlines of his gleaming, bronzed muscles. She felt her nipples grow taut again. Her hands snaked down between their bodies. The heat and hardness of him made her gasp with rekindled passion.

She arched her body, sinking down onto him, exhilarated by the feel of him filling her again. Slowly, tantalizingly, she moved in a circular motion. Lifting herself again so that he was poised on the edge of a dangerous, alluring crevice, she continued teasing him, arousing him, watching him as he watched her. And then, as if their lovemaking had been choreographed to be a perfect pas de deux, they shuddered in unison, eyes closing, Rafe reaching for her, drawing her to him fully. Her heart was hammering, an indescribable burning heat searing her loins. Then it felt as if the hot sun were bursting inside of her, and at the same moment, Rafe bringing them both to an elation and ecstasy beyond description.

Afterward they kissed, long and passionately. Then

138

Rachel rolled off him and curled up close to him, one arm beneath her head, the other between her thighs.

Rafe stroked the length of her body. "You used to sleep this way . . . like a child. So sweet." He smiled tenderly, letting his hand rest lightly on her hipbone. "Josh isn't the only one who's a wee bit drunk," he said with a sigh. "I feel drunk myself."

Rachel smiled, her blue eyes huge and sparkling. "Does that mean you find me intoxicating?"

He squeezed her flesh. "Inebriating."

"I'm hungry," she murmured, moving closer to him.

He gave her a look of astonishment.

She giggled. "For breakfast." She moved onto her back, stretching languorously. "I want a huge breakfast. Steak and eggs, pancakes, bacon . . ."

"Orange juice?" Rafe grinned.

Rachel twisted her body, concluding her sensual stretch against him. "Fresh-squeezed."

"Of course."

"I love you, Rafe," she said so naturally that only after she'd said it did she suddenly feel vulnerable. She looked away, unable to meet his gaze.

Rafe lifted her face to his and kissed her lightly on the lips. He looked at her, his eyes bright. "You see, some things never change; they endure."

She let out a ragged sob, throwing her arms around him, opening her mouth against his, their tongues making electric contact.

He eased her gently away. "Breakfast, remember?"

Rachel nodded. She felt more than a wee bit drunk herself.

He kissed the tip of her nose. "I'll take care of the food order. You meet me down at the cove. We'll eat and then take a sail over to our secret hideaway. It deserves a second chance, don't you think?"

"Absolutely," she whispered, a giddy smile on her face.

Twenty minutes later she laughed delightedly as Rafe appeared at the cove carrying a huge tray of breakfast treats. He'd dug up an old chef's hat and had placed it jauntily on his head. There was even the requisite white cloth draped formally over his arm. Beyond those accessories, all he wore were skimpy dark blue bathing trunks.

He gave Rachel a mischievous smile as he took in the sexy white bikini she was wearing. "I was going to tramp down here naked"—he grinned, setting the tray on the blanket that Rachel had spread out, his hat toppling off—"but I remembered we weren't alone on the island."

"Any stirrings from Norah's room?" Rachel lifted a slice of bacon and took a bite.

"Only snoring." He caught her wrist, took the rest of the bacon, and finished it off.

"What about Ned and Liz? They seem to have vanished into the blue."

Rafe nodded. "Apt description. I saw them out on the water in the motorboat."

"Don't tell me they're on the road to reconciliation

too?" Rachel looked over at Rafe, distraught to see a shadow pass over his features. "This *is* a reconciliation . . . isn't it?"

He took her hand, pressed it against his cheek, and smiled. But the shadow did not pass completely. The sky seemed to mirror Rafe's mood, suddenly growing bleak as the sun slipped behind a thick gray cloud. Rachel felt chilled, but it was far more Rafe's doing than the weather's.

She pulled her hand away. "Doesn't it mean anything to you?" she asked harshly, incredulously. "It does, damn it. I know it does."

"Of course it does, Rachel. I . . . never felt so much a part of you as I do now."

She felt as if a great, crushing weight had been lifted. An effervescent smile curved her lips. "Phew. You had me trembling there for a minute, Mr. Kincaid."

"Our breakfast is getting cold," he said, making a concerted effort to be light and playful. "I didn't want to hang around for steak to cook, but fortunately Lois had pancake batter all made up, bacon still warm, and eggs, sunny-side up, just the way you like it." He fed her a triangle of pancake.

"Mmmm. You're too slow," she said as he meticulously began cutting up another piece for her.

He squeezed her bottom. "You didn't complain about that before."

"True. Very true," she mumbled between voracious mouthfuls. She stabbed her fork into his plate, lifting up a large piece of egg. "Here. You're barely eating. Aren't you hungry?"

He took the proffered bite, shaking his head. "You more than took care of my appetite," he said seductively.

Rachel laughed. "I must be insatiable."

His palm trailed her thigh. "I like you that way."

She set her empty plate back on the tray and sighed contentedly, then polished off the large glass of freshly squeezed orange juice. Rafe shoved the tray off the blanket, and Rachel stretched out, resting her head on Rafe's bare leg. "Oh, Rafe, I feel so happy, so incredibly happy."

She smiled up at him, and he bent low and kissed her lips. Again she saw that fleeting shadow skim across his face. "What is it? What's wrong?" She hesitated. "Is it that photojournalist you left back in Nicaragua?"

He smiled tenderly, stroking her cheek. "Gwen Royce is my coworker, Rachel, not my lover. I'm afraid I used her to make you a touch jealous."

"A touch?" She tugged his hair, pulling his face to hers. "It was torment . . . sheer torment imagining you were in love with another woman."

"There hasn't been another woman, Rach," he said softly, his lips brushing her cheek.

"There's been no one special in my life, either, Rafe. At first it seemed unimaginable that I could even think of falling in love again. And then later, when the loneliness and emptiness simply wouldn't go away, I tried desperately to fall in love. I wanted someone to lift the pain, to make me feel alive again, to make me feel like a woman. Only . . . no one could do that for me. No one. It's always been you, Rafe. Always."

He lifted her, cradling her in his arms, kissing her eyes, her nose, her cheeks, her lips.

"Oh, Rafe, what happens now?"

He held her tightly. "I don't know, Rachel."

She was clinging to him, her head pressed against his shoulder, her face hidden by her tousled hair. "We could . . . get married again." She held her breath, waiting. But there was no answer from Rafe. Her breath came out in a painful explosion. She pulled away, her eyes searching his. She tried to smile. "You did propose the last time. I thought it was my turn."

"Rachel . . ."

"You don't want to get married again do you?" Her voice was raspy; she was finding it incredibly hard to breathe. "Do you?" This time her voice was a painful cry.

"Rachel, listen to me." He grabbed her shoulders. "I don't want us to make the same mistake twice, that's all."

"I see," she said stiffly, wrenching free of his grasp, scrambling to her feet.

"No, you don't see," he said harshly. "You want to do the same thing again, rush in without thinking, without trying to understand—"

"Oh, I understand," she said, cutting him off sharply. "I understand that you're a man who lives for

143

the moment, right? You like your freedom. You grab at life, Rafe. You're a taker. A selfish, grabbing hustler. You love taking photos because you can be a voyeur . . . always on the outside snatching glimpses, then moving on. And like a fool I let you glimpse into my heart . . . into my soul." She spun around, racing for the sailboat docked in the cove. She had to get off the island. She had to get away. The pain was so bad, it was engulfing her.

Rafe ran after her and grabbed her. "You've got it wrong, Rachel. Damn it, I love you; you've got to know that. It's just . . . I don't want to put either of us through that pain again." He grasped her shoulders. He was shaking her hard, his own rage surfacing, consuming him. "Marriage didn't work for us, Rachel. We both went through torture afterward. Don't you see what I'm telling you?"

"What you're telling me," Rachel murmured coldly, "is that you're a coward. Let go of me, Rafe. I hate myself for loving you. You told me I was the one running away. But it's you. You're terrified of your feelings. You'd rather take pictures of other people's pain, joy, fear, desire . . . than truly feel those emotions yourself." She broke loose of him and raced to the boat.

Rafe let her go. He shut his eyes. But he couldn't block out the misery that fell over him like a shroud. He had tried to make her understand, but he knew she didn't. Maybe he didn't really understand, himself. All he knew was that the one time he'd opened himself fully, impulsively, to love, it had nearly suffocated him. He'd had no business marrying Rachel in the first place. It had been sheer madness.

He laughed dryly to himself. Sheer madness. Rachel's years on that dumb game show had obviously inured her to the panic that madness wrought. Rafe found it overwhelming. He found Rachel overwhelming. The love he felt so fiercely for her, he found most overwhelming of all.

Rachel guided the boat toward the small island. At first she'd meant to go straight to the coast, but for one thing, the sea was getting very rough as the sky continued to darken; for another, all she had on was her skimpy bikini. The motor churned loudly over the choppy waves, but Rachel was oblivious to the increasing rockiness as the boat heaved precariously over each swell. Her pain obliterated any sign of danger. All she could think of was that she'd lost him once more. Her mind flooded with recriminations. The crazy thing was, despite it all, she knew she would do it over again. Even the hurt did nothing to diminish the incredible joy she and Rafe had shared. Now she was left to pay the price.

It was only when the dark clouds broke open suddenly, and bullets of rain tumbled fiercely down from the sky that Rachel pulled herself out of her emotional misery and realized the serious peril she was in.

Besides the rain pelting down, the giant swells forced water over first one side of the boat and then the other. Rachel could barely see ahead of her. She had no idea how close she'd gotten to the small island. Terror gripped her as the boat teetered almost over onto its side, the gusting winds pounding the wooden frame. Rachel clung to the mast after making sure the boom was fastened securely with line so it wouldn't swing out and smash her into the turbulent sea. Her mind flashed on Rafe, the vision so clear that it gave her strange comfort in the midst of her horror. No, she had no regrets. None. She'd given him all she had to give. The gift of herself, her love.

Thunder exploded around her. Rachel held on tightly, eyes shut, clinging to that image of Rafe, praying. . . .

Suddenly the boat crashed up against a barrier. For a moment Rachel thought it had hit one of the sandbars. If so, she stood little chance of making it to shore on her own steam. The water would capture her, consume her.

Then she realized that it wasn't a sandbar. It was the shoreline. The boat had washed up on the shore of the deserted island. Rachel clambered out of the boat, falling onto the wet sand, crying, laughing, taking in gulps of air and rain at the same time.

Ned and Liz had to use all of their combined strength to physically hold Rafe back from taking out another boat and going in search of Rachel.

"You can't go out in this storm, Rafe," Ned shouted. "It's pure insanity. It's suicide."

146

"Look, she must have made it to the other island before it got too rough out there," Liz jumped in.

"Let go of me, dammit. I've got to get to her."

"That's crazy talk, man. You'll never make it. Face it, for chrissake," Ned said, his voice intentionally harsh. "You won't get to her no matter where the hell she is. All you'll succeed in doing is getting yourself killed. What good is that going to do Rachel?"

Rafe wouldn't listen to them. He was far beyond reason. Oh, God, Rachel, be all right. Please be all right. He wrenched free of their grasp, taking a solid punch at Ned that sent him sprawling to the ground. Liz, not about to hold him back on her own and not wanting to taste that fist, backed up as Rafe darted for the boat they'd brought in a short while ago.

Liz helped Ned to his feet as they listened to the spurt of the motor. "He's never going to make it," she murmured in the storm.

"I doubt that Rachel did, either," Ned whispered in a pained voice.

They ran back to the house. They'd alert the coast guard and they'd have to tell Josh and Norah.

The sea raged. Rafe, a superb sailor, had been in rough storms before, but this was more than an ordinary storm; he knew it was a prelude to a hurricane, which meant that even if Rachel had somehow, incredibly, made it to the other island, she was still in great danger. That cottage could easily be smashed to pieces in a bad hurricane.

147

The boat pitched violently in the treacherous sea, dipping low, then rising up like a wild, foaming mare. Several times Rafe was thrown down to the floor of the boat by the swirling winds. A deluge of water cascaded over the sides. Rafe was cold, his body shivering, but his mind was on one thing only, making it to that island . . . finding Rachel. She was his lifeline, his strength, his love.

It seemed an eternity in hell before he neared shore and was able to make out the silhouette of Rachel's boat, upturned and battered, on the shore. He broke out in a loud sob of relief. She was here. She'd made it.

Then suddenly the hurricane hit full force. Just on the edge of safety, a huge swell caught him unaware, and he was thrown into the sea.

The icy, clawing water spiraled around him, dragging him down, the rocky bottom scraping and cutting his chest. He tumbled in its grasp, dizzied, striking blindly for shore.

He broke the surface, gasping and coughing. He tried to shake his eyes clear of the stinging salt water so that he could get a clear fix on the shoreline, the sea having turned him every which way so that he had lost all sense of direction.

It was impossible to see more than a few yards in front of him. Diving down into the water of his own accord this time, he knew he'd have to trust to his senses. Cloying at the rocks on the surface of the sea about six feet below, he pulled himself along. His lungs burned fiercely as he held his breath, moving relentlessly as the undertow fought against him. But that undertow was his friend as well as his enemy. It let him know he was moving in the right direction.

At last he hit shallow water and broke through to the surface. He struggled to rise as his body came into contact with the smooth, sandy base, but his legs wouldn't hold him. The cruel wind and stinging rain smashed at him. He used his very last ounce of strength to pull himself like a beached whale onto the shore. Gasping, his pupils rolled up in his head and he passed out.

Rachel listened to the raging storm from inside the cottage. She'd thrown an old robe over her, but she still felt chilled. And then she thought about the boat, pulled carelessly onto shore. She'd been so relieved at making it to the island, she'd left the boat without securing it in any way. There was nothing to prevent it from being swept back to sea.

Fear made her hesitate. The storm was growing worse. It was rattling the windows. The shutters had come completely loose, and she could see one of them being tossed about as if it were made of paper. But she found herself becoming obsessed by the boat, knowing that she had to get back down to the beach, make sure it was there, that it was all right. She had to secure it. Ripping off the robe, she threw on an old slicker from the hall closet. When she opened the door, it flew against her, nearly knocking the wind from her. But she was resolute. She crossed her arms in front of her and lowered her head, bucking the wind and the lash-ing rain.

Had she known all along that he was in danger? Had there been some deep, inner force that had, in truth, driven her down to the shore? Rachel didn't know. All she knew was that when she saw him stretched out unconscious on the sand, she was not at all surprised to find him there—terrified that he'd been seriously hurt but, for some inexplicable reason, not surprised in the least that he had come for her.

She knelt down beside him, immediately administer-ing artificial respiration. For several long minutes she feared she wouldn't be able to revive him. But then suddenly he gasped, and his eyes fluttered open. She stroked his head, kissed him, cried with happiness.

His hand lifted weakly to her face. "Are you all right?" he whispered.

She fell against him. "I am now. I am now."

CHAPTER NINE

"The boat house," Rafe shouted over the cacophony of rain and wind. "There's a cellar there."

"Couldn't we wait it out at the cottage?" Rachel clung to him as the storm raged, attacking them from all sides.

Rafe's arm tightened around her. He couldn't hear what she was saying, but her terror was palpable. "It's going to be okay, baby." He clutched her. "We made it this far."

The small shed that Rachel had equated yesterday with something out of a horror film, was even more ominous now. Howling gusts of wind tore through the dark, dank, cluttered space. Rain poured down from a half dozen holes in the roof. Rachel felt cold, murky water rise up around her ankles. Bile rose in her throat.

"Rachel," Rafe shouted harshly, seeing in the dim, shadowed light that she was on the verge of having a panic attack. "Help me lift these two boats out of the way. There's a trapdoor just underneath."

Rachel gripped the edge of the boat numbly, but then an ominous creaking sound made her freeze.

"Watch out," Rafe screamed, grabbing her arm, shoving her against the side wall of the shed seconds before a huge chunk of the roof came crashing down on her.

She moaned, a paralyzing fear gripping her. *We're going to die,* she thought. *We're going to die.*

But Rafe Kincaid hadn't come this far to give it all up now. "Damn it, Rachel, stop acting like a child. Pull yourself together." He wrenched her in the direction of the boat. "Come on."

She looked at him with wide, frightened eyes, but she did as he commanded. When she saw him wince in pain as they tugged the second boat onto its side, it brought Rachel sharply back to life.

"Let me," she pleaded as Rafe tugged on the trapdoor, trying to lift it. But Rafe shrugged her off, despite the grimace of pain etching the lines of his face.

The door finally gave way. "Okay. Go ahead," he ordered.

Rachel stared into the dark cavity. Once again logic —which told her that everything, including her and Rafe, could be blown to kingdom come if they didn't find safe shelter—succumbed to fear, the terrifying images of grotesque snakes, rats and who-knew-what other hideous creatures crawling below making her freeze.

"Don't be afraid, Rachel." The timbre of Rafe's voice had changed; the harshness was gone. Soothing hands caressed her shoulders, suffusing her with courage. "I'll go first," he said, giving her a reassuring squeeze.

Quickly he stepped down into the ten-by-fifteen space, a low cellar less than six feet high. Rafe, at six foot two inches, had to keep his head bent as he reached up for Rachel. He guided her down the rickety ladder, gathering her in his arms.

"Oh, Rafe, how could I have been so stupid?" she murmured, chastising herself hotly as he held her tightly to him.

He kissed her softly. As his eyes became acclimated to the darker space he saw the fear, anxiety, and guilt in her beautiful, dark blue eyes. "No use worrying about anything now. We'll be fine here until this squall blows over. Relax," he said as she looked cautiously down around their feet for anything that might go bump in the storm. "I won't let anything nip you."

Rachel cast him a winsome smile. "You're a real hero, Rafe Kincaid. But you shouldn't have come after me. First I pull a dumb stunt, and then you go compounding it."

"What's one more little dumb stunt between . . . a pair of crazy lovers like us?" he asked gently.

"We are crazy," she said, sighing. "I don't know which one of us has a worse case of sheer madness." She touched his scraped jaw, a tremor in her voice. "You could have gotten yourself killed."

He kissed her passionately. "You know I'd die for you, Rachel."

"So, I guess I'm to conclude . . . that marriage, in

your book, must be a fate worse than death." But her attempt at humor fell flat.

"Isn't this where we left off?"

"You'd think I'd have acquired a bit more pride over the years, along with my stubbornness, determination, and womanly figure." She laughed dryly. "But after all we've been through since we set eyes on each other again, maybe pride is superfluous."

He tilted her head in his direction. "You've got something more valuable than pride, Rach. You've got class. Real class."

She gave him a devilish smile. "And you mean to tell me the classiest photojournalist in the world is going to let an ex-wife outclass him?"

He smoothed her hair back, then lowered his mouth to hers. "You have always outclassed me, Rachel. Just as you have always haunted me." His close gaze took in every detail of her features in the dimness.

Rachel felt a fevered heat coupled with an immeasurable sadness. "Rafe, we still love each other. We . . . could take a chance. We're older . . ."

"Older but not necessarily wiser, darling." His eyes skidded off her face. "You said it yourself, Rachel. I haven't changed. I don't know if I can set down roots, raise a family, give you what you want—what you have every right to want—any more now than I could five years ago."

"Rafe . . ." But before she could go on there was a horrendous noise. It sounded as if the world had come to an end. Shingles, boards, and crates began raining down on them. Rafe grabbed Rachel, falling over her protectively on the cold, hard floor while the remainder of the shed collapsed over them, sealing them into the wet, dark cellar.

When he was certain that the building had stopped showering down on them, he eased off Rachel.

"Are you okay?" he asked breathlessly.

He got onto his bare knees, the dank, damp air making him shiver. He didn't want to think that being trapped in this hellhole was adding to his chill. "Rachel . . ."

He couldn't see a thing as he reached out for her. "Rachel?"

His hand touched her hair. He lifted her head. It fell limply against his chest. Panic hit him as she moaned softly. His hand brushed her hair from her face, and he felt something warm and sticky close to her temple: blood.

He opened her slicker, reaching around to unfasten the bra of her bikini. It was little more than a handkerchief, but it would have to do. Working in the blackness, he put pressure by the wound to stem the bleeding as best he could, then wrapped the band, pirate-fashion, around her head. She'd passed out in the meantime. He gently laid her down and climbed up the ladder, desperately trying to make an opening in the debris. The cellar was no longer their source of safety. It had become a living tomb.

Breathless with pain and exertion, Rafe tried to tear away the barrier. Twice he lost his footing and went

155

crashing to the ground. He was getting nowhere fast. When he heard Rachel call his name, he gave up the near hopeless task and went to her.

"It's all right, darling," he crooned. "You're all right."

"Rafe . . . I'm sorry." She was shivering, and he rubbed her arms and legs down vigorously, then cradled her against him.

"I love you, Rachel. I love you so very much. Don't worry, darling. We'll get out of this mess."

"If . . . if we don't . . . I just want you to know . . . I've endlessly regretted that day in my office five years ago. As soon as you walked out that door . . . I so desperately wanted to call you back. Funny thing . . . about pride. It strikes so unpredictably. I've never stopped . . . loving you."

He rocked her in his arms, listening to her quickening breath, knowing that they had only a few hours at most before there would be no more air left. He stroked her, tenderly saying that they'd make it, wanting to assure her, wanting to assure himself as well. His own breathing was raw, every muscle in his body aching. He felt Rachel go limp beside him, knew that she had blacked out again. He carefully laid her back down and resumed the near futile task of trying to clear a way to freedom.

He had no idea how much time had passed when he fell back against the wall, fighting for breath. He felt certain that the whole damn shed must have landed on that hole. Robbed of strength, lacking any tools, he knew the task was hopeless. He heard Rachel's shallow breathing and crawled over to her. He touched the makeshift bandanna over her head and felt the wet spot where the blood had saturated through the cloth.

"Rachel, I love you. If you can hear me, Rachel . . . forgive me." He held her tenderly in his arms. "Oh, Rachel, you aren't the only one who regretted that awful confrontation in your office. I was so hot-headed that day. And proud. So damn proud. I went a little crazy when I came home that morning and found you gone. When I saw you and you told me it was over, I still couldn't really believe it. Even when I walked out . . . I couldn't get it through my thick skull that we were finished. When it finally sank in, I wanted to turn around, march back in there, grab you in my arms and tell you . . . that . . . that you were the most important thing in my life . . . that you were . . . my roots. You were all I wanted, Rachel."

He felt her stir again. He kissed her lightly. "Hold on, baby. Hold on."

"Rafe . . ."

"Shhh. Don't talk now. We'll have plenty of time. . . ." Plenty of time. Never before had time seemed so tenuous, nor so precious to him. "I love you, Rachel. If . . . when we get out of here, we'll work something out. I promise. Do you hear me, Rachel?"

"Promises were made to be . . . broken," she said in a low voice.

"There are exceptions to every rule," he said softly. Suddenly he grew alert. "Rachel, did you hear that?"

157

"Something about promises?"

"No, no. Outside. I thought I heard someone calling our names." As he was speaking, they both distinctly heard voices.

"Here," Rafe shouted. "We're here under the shed in the cellar."

"Are you okay?" It was Josh, and there was no missing the combination of relief and tension in his voice.

"Hurry, Josh!"

"I've got a couple of coast guardsmen with me. Ned is here too. We'll have you dug out as quickly as we can. Just hold on, Rafe."

It took nearly an hour to finally clear the trapdoor opening. Rafe allowed Josh to help him get Rachel up from the cellar, but once they were in the open air again, he refused to let anyone else take charge of her despite his own pain and exhaustion.

The storm had tempered and the coast guard crawler had little difficulty cutting across the water. Rafe and Rachel were given dry clothes, and one of the sailors, who had had medical training, expertly bandaged Rachel's wound. The bleeding had stopped, and she was fully conscious but drained. The sailors went back on deck to attend to the ship, and Josh and Ned, after making sure that Rachel and Rafe were okay, followed discretely. They got the distinct impression the two wanted to be by themselves.

"Fresh air has a remarkably curative effect," Rachel

proclaimed, taking in a deep breath once they were alone.

Rafe smiled at her, thinking her the most beautiful creature he'd ever laid eyes on, even in the oversize sweatshirt and jeans borrowed from one of the sailors. But there were still lines of worry etching his features. "Rachel, you were out cold for quite a while. I think we should have you checked out at a hospital."

"I wasn't out that cold, Rafe Kincaid. I heard all about how you felt that day in my office five years ago." Her eyes sparkled. "I also heard you promise that we were going to work something out."

"You heard all that, did you?"

She laughed softly. "Every last word."

"You could have been hallucinating," he said, teasing.

She wrapped her arms around his neck. "I may be a fool, Rafe, but I'm not fool enough to let you out of my life again."

His hands moved around her waist, slipping up and under the sweatshirt to her warmed skin. "I'm not that big a fool to let that happen." He hesitated for a fraction of a moment. "Do I get a second chance on that proposal, Miss Mason?"

Rachel held her breath, tears misting her eyes. "You're not just feeling . . . I mean, with all that's happened . . . coming so close to . . . to dying . . ." She took a gulp of air.

He gave her a tender smile. "Maybe we could make it a double wedding."

Rachel's eyes studied his face closely. She sniffed. "No."

"No? No, what? No double wedding? Or no wedding at all?"

Rachel's lips compressed. "I think we need to think things through. You said yourself—"

Rafe slammed the heel of his hand against his forehead. "I don't believe I'm hearing right," he said harshly. "After practically *begging* me to marry you—"

"Damn you, Rafe Kincaid. I didn't beg. How dare you—"

"You heard me. Beg. And now you're the one getting cold feet? That's beautiful, Rachel. That's really one for the books."

"You were the one who said we shouldn't rush into marriage again. You were the one who said you probably never would have married me in the first place if . . . if I'd been a . . . a slut like the rest of the women you obviously were used to being with."

"Slut? Oh, you weren't a slut, that's for sure. You were the biggest damn prude to hit the twentieth century. You were straight out of the Victorian era, you were."

"Just because I happened to have some pride—"

"Pride, my eye. You were wangling for a wedding ring right from the start. You played little Miss Don't Touch, so that I'd be fool enough to drag myself down the altar."

"And what's your excuse now for being willing to

drag yourself down again? You certainly can't claim I was a prude this time around."

Rafe suddenly broke out laughing. Rachel, despite her weakness, tried to lash out at him, but he captured her hand and brought it to his lips. Then he leaned toward her and brought his lips to hers. Rachel was too stunned by his abrupt shift to say anything at all. He took advantage of the silence to kiss her fully on the mouth.

When at last he released her, she eyed him warily. "Are you trying to tell me something?"

He took her in his arms. "Let's do it, Rachel. Let's get married. Think how dull life will be if we don't."

"You've got a point there, Kincaid." She felt her heart beating wildly. "A double wedding, huh? That would be something." She laughed softly. Then she pulled herself away. "If Josh and Norah agree, of course. It is their day. If our sneaky prank worked, that is—and they've made up." She pressed her hands to her heart. "It would be lovely. My folks will be here. They never did understand, my mother especially, how I could have let you go." She stopped short. "We're doing exactly what we did before, aren't we? Rushing into marriage. What about the future, Rafe? Do we get a second honeymoon or will you be trouping back to Nicaragua, telephoto lens in hand? Do we buy that house in Connecticut? Do we start a family? If I'm in labor at the hospital, will you be there by my side doing deep-breathing exercises with me, or will you be off in Tasmania or Bangkok or Seoul?"

"Slow down, Rachel," Rafe said with an easy smile, which, in truth, did not come at all easy. Rachel was raising some important questions, and he wasn't sure of any of the answers. "We'll take it one step at a time."

An uneasiness flickered in Rachel's eyes. "All right. I guess the important thing is . . . we love each other."

He drew her into his arms. "That is an undisputed fact, darling." He swept her hair off her face, gently kissing her temple just below the bandage. "Are you in a lot of pain?"

She deliberately brightened. "No little battle wound is going to ruin my happiness."

"You look very sexy as a wounded soldier of fortune, Miss Mason. And"—he leaned closer, slipping his hand under her sweatshirt and grazing her breast —"I owe you a new bikini."

She put her arms around him. "I owe you my life," she whispered. "If you hadn't come for me . . ." She shut her eyes tightly. As Rafe had carried her out of the boat house Rachel had seen that the cottage had been severely damaged by the storm, one whole section of roof having caved in.

He held her tightly. He, too, knew that Rachel could have very likely been in that part of the cottage that had collapsed. The thought that he could have lost her was intolerable.

162

"Oh, Rachel, I love you," he murmured. Then he held her at arm's length and gave her a warm, tender smile. "How about Paris?"

"Paris?"

"For our honeymoon."

She eyed him warily. "You have an assignment coming up in Paris."

He grinned. "I do not have an assignment coming up in Paris." His smile faded. "We have a lot of lost time to make up for, Rachel. Paris, for one. Back five years, when I did have that assignment and went off to Paris, it was devastatingly lonely. I kept thinking how wonderful it would have been walking along the Champs-Elysée with you, sitting together in the cafés, going to the Louvre."

A small frown creased her brow. "Had I gone with you, I very likely would have been doing all of those things alone. You would have been busy working most of the time."

Rafe sighed. He didn't want to get into another argument with Rachel. "Well, my darling wife-to-be, this time we shall have a real second honeymoon. We'll stay in a romantic suite on the Left Bank, overlooking the Seine, of course. We'll feed each other croissants in the morning, embrace at the top of the Eiffel Tower in the afternoon, dine at Maxim's, go to the Folies Bergère, and last, but most definitely not least, we'll make wild, passionate love as the stars come out over the City of Lights."

Sensual shudders quivered over her skin, and a se-

ductive smile curved her lips. "Can we skip the pre-
liminaries occasionally and go directly to the part
about when the stars twinkle in the sky?"

He pulled Rachel to him and held her close, feeling
her heartbeat against his.

They were oblivious to the sound of the engines
shutting off in the boat. It was Josh who broke up
their hungry kiss.

"I see the two of you are no worse for wear," he
said teasingly.

Rachel grinned. "I'd say we've pulled through the
crisis quite nicely."

As Rafe, Rachel, Josh, and Ned disembarked, Norah and Liz came running up to the dock.

Norah gasped when she saw Rachel's bandaged
head, but Rachel quickly assured her sister that it was
a minor wound.

"Rachel, I was worried sick," Norah said breath-
lessly, giving the whole group a sweeping glance.
"About all of you. I was afraid no one would survive."
Her voice trembled.

Liz compressed her lips, fighting back tears. She
said very little, but Rachel noticed that her eyes did
not leave Ned for very long.

Rachel hugged Norah, then led her off, ahead of the
others. After Rachel filled her in on what had happened on the island, up to and including the rescue
mission, she whispered, "Is everything all right between you and Josh?"

Norah kissed her sister's cheek. "That was a nasty

little trick you played on us. I nearly jumped out of my skin when I woke up to find myself entwined around the body of my supposedly *ex*-fiancé."

Rachel looked sheepish, but Norah smiled brightly. "I never knew a man could be so passionate and loving while suffering from a fierce hangover," Norah said with a happy laugh.

"I'm so relieved. Besides"—Rachel paused—"we couldn't very well consider a double wedding if you and Josh—"

"A double . . ." Norah's eyes widened in merry astonishment. "You don't mean . . . you and Rafe?"

Rachel gave a quick glance over her shoulder. "I'm afraid he's the only available bachelor around. Ned and Liz seem to have ironed a few things out themselves."

Norah glanced back too. Ned and Liz had stayed back by the dock. They seemed mindless of the rain that was still coming down quite heavily as they fell into each others' arms. Norah clapped her hands delightedly, giving Rafe and Josh, who were coming up behind them, cheery winks.

When they got to the house, Norah went upstairs with Rachel while the two brothers headed straight for the library.

"Isn't life wonderful?" Norah sighed, squeezing her sister's shoulder as they stepped inside Rachel's room. "To be honest with you, Rachel, I was worried about how things would work out with you and Rafe—with Liz and Ned as well."

"For a while there we were all courting disaster," Rachel admitted with a devilish smile. "It quite surpassed any amount of insanity I've ever witnessed on my game show."

"But look how things worked out in the end," Norah said with a grin. "It appears that getting married must be contagious."

Rachel went into the bathroom to shower, and Norah leaned against the sink to continue their conversation.

"Do you think I'm doing the right thing, Norah?" Rachel shouted over the steamy thunder, keeping her head tilted back so as not to wet the bandage on her forehead.

"Do any of us ever really know the answer to that question?"

Rachel stuck her head out of the corner of the curtain. "You don't regret mending things with Josh, do you?"

Norah looked thoughtful. "No. No, I don't regret it. But I don't have any illusions about everything working out easily. Marriage is hard work. Both Josh and I are going to have to struggle with . . . a lot of issues. But we both feel it's worth the struggle."

A shadow fell across Rachel's face. "I don't imagine any two people will have more of a struggle than Rafe and I." She turned off the faucet and stepped out of the shower, wrapping a large white bath towel around her.

"I think there are some couples who are truly destined for one another, despite the conflicts, the battles, the struggles. You and Rafe are inexorably bound together, Rachel. You must both have come to realize that by now."

Rachel frowned as she stared at her reflection in the mirror. "You make it seem a bit more like we're doomed rather than fated to be together."

Norah gave her an affectionate squeeze. "Nonsense. I think you and Rafe are the most passionately romantic pair to have hit the twentieth century."

Rachel took hold of her sister's hands as she turned around to face her. "If it doesn't work out this time between us, I don't think I could bare it. I do love him so desperately, Norah. And I think we both know that we'll have to make . . . some changes." She smiled brightly through tears. "We're going to Paris on our honeymoon. Strictly pleasure. Rafe swears there is no assignment involved." She hugged her sister fiercely, the tears flowing freely now. "I want everything to work out, Norah. I've never wanted anything so much in my life. He mustn't leave me again. He mustn't."

"He won't, darling." Norah wiped away her sister's tears. "Now, listen to me, Rachel Mason. You have no more time for tears, fears, or pranks. Time to buckle down. We have scads of work ahead of us if we're going to pull off the double wedding of the century. For starters you need a wedding dress."

Rachel grinned. "I already thought of that. Really, my maid of honor dress will do perfectly. We can have your dressmaker do a few minor changes and I'll be set. After all, a divorced woman doesn't wed in white. All we really need is to fit another happy bride and groom on top of the wedding cake."

"Wait until Mom and Dad hear the news. And the Kincaids," Norah said excitedly. "Oh, Rachel, everyone is going to be ecstatic. Do you know that except for you and Rafe, everyone else in the world has known all along that you were meant for each other? It's about time you both came to your senses."

Rachel wiped away a few more errant tears. "When I think of all the time we wasted . . ."

Norah touched her cheek. "Don't look back, Rachel. Just look ahead to your future together."

Rachel nodded brightly, although she continued to experience an unsettling feeling about her future with Rafe. He'd said they would take things one step at a time. The first time around, their steps had led them in two very divergent directions.

But as she opened the bathroom door and saw Rafe stretched out on the bed, waiting for her, a lazy, loving look in his eyes, Rachel's doubts faded.

Norah made a fast exit after giving her sister and her future brother-in-law a broad smile. Neither of them noticed; their eyes were locked on each other.

Rachel stood motionless as Norah shut the door.

"Come here," Rafe commanded, patting the bed beside him.

"Don't you think you're being a bit presumptuous?" she said teasingly. "Think about our upcoming wedding night."

He gave her a warm, seductive smile. "I've been thinking about it for the past five years."

Her eyes sparkled as she walked slowly toward him . . . one step at a time.

CHAPTER TEN

"I love weddings." Rachel grinned, swirling around in her silk fuchsia jacquard gown.

"You look fantastic," Norah exclaimed, then studied her own face more closely in the three-sided mirror. "I can only attribute your radiance to the fact that you've been through it once already." She frowned at a small blemish on her chin. "I think I have premarital acne."

Rachel grinned. "Your skin is perfect. You're perfect. Your husband-to-be is perfect." She did another pirouette, then observed her own reflection in the mirror. "Life is perfect," she declared with an expansive sigh.

Norah tugged on the pinned-up seam of Rachel's gown. "Well, this gown won't be perfect if you don't take it off and give it back to Naomi to finish up. Four more days, Rachel."

Rachel cocked her head. "For heaven's sake, Norah, you make it sound like four days until . . . execution."

Norah turned away. "For some reason I lack your absolute optimism." She rummaged in her bag for a tissue. "Oh, God," she said, sniffling, "my allergies have never been worse."

Rachel rested her hands on Norah's shoulders. "It's natural to be frightened," she said softly.

"You're not."

"Probably because I'm a fool."

"No," Norah was quick to say. "You aren't a fool. You've simply had years of knowing that you are deeply, unabidingly in love with Rafe Kincaid."

"And you're not in love with Josh?"

"Of course I am," Norah said. "But it's a matter of how strong that love is." She turned and faced Rachel. "You and Rafe have been through both heaven and hell together. You've endured." She shrugged. "Look at Liz and Ned. For a while there I actually thought they'd make it."

Rachel eyed Norah shrewdly. "That's really what your panic is all about. Just because Ned and Liz split up again has nothing to do with you and Josh. Besides, I wouldn't be too quick to write that relationship off."

"I suppose you're right. I've never been particularly superstitious, but right now every little incident seems portentous."

"Well," Rachel said emphatically, "I absolutely refuse to look on the dark side. And since we're tripping merrily down that aisle together on Sunday, I want you to be as starry-eyed and optimistic as I am. Agreed?"

Norah grinned. "Agreed."

When Rachel and Norah returned to the island that afternoon from their fittings in Greenwich, the house was swarming with people. Liz had brought her crew of four down to complete the decorating, the florist was checking on the table arrangements, friends and relatives from out of town were filling up the guest rooms, and the caterer was conferring with Ellen Kincaid about the wedding supper.

Ellen Kincaid, a slender, impeccably dressed woman with beautifully coiffed dark hair that gave her maturing features a touch of youthful elegance, looked up with a harried smile as the two sisters walked into the library. Rachel felt a small twinge of guilt knowing that transforming the ceremony into a double wedding had made more work for everyone, especially Rafe's mother, Ellen. Then again, Ellen Kincaid had literally cried with joy when she and Rafe had announced their plans to marry again and had brought up the idea of the double affair even before Rachel had a chance to say that was what they wanted to do.

"Oh, darlings," Ellen exclaimed, breaking off her conversation with the caterer, "do see if Lois can spare some time from her dinner preparations to come in here and talk with Monsieur Beauchamp."

Monsieur Beauchamp, the head caterer, was busily going through his portfolio of papers and gave the two sisters an impatient nod. "It is too much . . . all zees changes, madam."

Ellen raised a brow and shrugged, giving Rachel a

bright smile. "Oh, dear, I almost forgot, Rachel," Ellen said as she and Norah were walking out. "Rafe is at the outer island doing some repairs on the cottage. He wanted you to go over and join him when you got home."

"I'll go inform Lois that Monsieur is awaiting her appearance," Norah said with an exaggerated French accent when they stepped out of the library and shut the door. "You, mademoiselle, must hurry off to your *amour.*"

"I don't believe for an instant that Rafe is out there mending the cottage." Rachel smiled. "He's simply hiding out from the herd. I can't blame him. If one more relative winks at me and tells me that it was a shame to have gone through the expense and bother of a divorce, I swear I'm going to—"

"Temper, temper," Norah said, laughing. "Where's that sunny disposition, that unbounding cheeriness and optimism?"

"I need rejuvenation. As you say, sister dear, *mon amour* awaits."

Rachel changed into a silver-and-white bikini, threw a cover-up over it, and took a small Sailfish out to meet Rafe. When she arrived at the tiny island, she saw him stretched out on the sand at the cove.

"Your mother informed me you were busily repairing the cottage," Rachel said, dropping onto the blanket beside him. "Playing hooky?"

He squinted up at her. "I needed some excuse to get away. That place is a madhouse."

She bent low and kissed his lips, running her tongue across his mouth. "Salty."

"I've been swimming." He closed his eyes, head tilted up to the sun. "I'd like to stay out here until they call us to walk down the aisle. We could hop into our formal attire, run over, say our I dos, and make a quick getaway."

Rachel lifted the terry cover-up over her head and stretched out beside Rafe, curving against his warm body. "Mmmm. That sounds like a great idea. Let's throw a tarp over the roof of the cottage and camp out here until Sunday afternoon."

When Rafe didn't answer, Rachel propped her head in her hand and gazed down at him. "You seem a bit glum," Rachel said softly after a few moments. "Wedding plans have you down?" She hesitated. "Or the wedding itself?"

He gave her a sidelong glance. His eyes were shadowed. She heard him pull in his breath. "I got a wire from Gwen this morning."

"Gwen?" For a moment the name didn't ring a bell.

"My assistant," he clarified.

"Oh." Rachel said. "Is . . . is everything . . . all right?"

He ran his tongue over his salty lips. "There was a skirmish that got a bit hairy, but she managed to get some fantastic shots. Or so she says." He gave Rachel a crooked grin. "I guess I'm suffering from a wounded ego. Funny how we go around thinking we're the only

174

ones that can get a job done right, that we're indispensable."

Rachel's fingers trailed down his chest. "You are indispensable to me."

He pulled her down into his arms and kissed her roughly. Rachel's mouth clung to his. Her muscles tensed. There was a hint of desperation in Rafe's kiss, in the way his hands moved down her body.

She leaned on her elbow again when he finally released her. "What is it, Rafe? Do you wish you were in Nicaragua, risking life and limb?"

He studied her carefully. "We haven't really resolved what's going to happen after the honeymoon, Rachel. I do have to earn a living, you know."

Rachel frowned. "There are plenty of photojournalists who make a perfectly good living without racing off to the far corners of the earth, unsure of whether the next picture they take might be their last."

He smoothed back her hair, studying her for a long moment. "I put in a call to Rob Holiday at *The New York Times Magazine*. He once told me if I ever got tired of packing and unpacking my bags to look him up."

Rachel's pulse quickened. "Oh, Rafe, that would be perfect. It's a great magazine. You always said that. And it would mean all local assignments." She threw her arms around his neck. "We really could set down roots, begin thinking of a family, maybe even do over the cottage here if your dad will sell us the island instead of selling it to his brother. This is our special place," she said with a soft smile.

Rafe kissed her tenderly. "Slow down, babe. I just put in a call. I didn't get the job yet. I'll go in and talk to him after we get back from Paris."

Rachel regarded him closely. "It's going to be a drastic change for you," she said slowly. "None of the danger and excitement . . ."

"I'll have to get my excitement elsewhere," he said seductively, letting his fingers trail along the bra top of her bikini.

Rachel smiled, but when her eyes met his, she still saw a flicker of brooding there.

"Come on. Let's take a swim," he said with a smile that Rachel thought was forced.

He stood up, pulling her into his arms and embracing her gently. When he released her, his smile was warm, tender, loving. "Last one in . . . throws the tarp on the cottage roof."

They raced into the water, laughing, the tension vanishing. Afterward they pulled the blanket off to a secluded spot on the cove and sank into each other's arms. Rafe quickly rid them both of their skimpy suits and arched her against him. Her eyes met his. The brooding look had returned, but now it was coupled with a fevered hunger. His mouth claimed hers hotly, his tongue thrusting into her mouth. His hands were rough and demanding over her body, a wild urgency in his every touch. She was stunned by his ferocity, but she found herself responding to his driving heat with a fire all her own.

Rachel's body writhed and twisted under his assault. Her pulse raced madly, her fingers raking through his hair as he took her with a possessive force that made her cry out. Mindless of the ruthlessness of Rafe's lovemaking, Rachel gave herself to him with total abandon. Her nails dug into his hard, muscled back as he took her with fierce, demanding thrusts. She gasped against him, her body quaking, head thrown back.

As the searing heat consumed them his lips descended on hers like a fiery demon. She groaned into his mouth, responding with a fury of her own, driven by a wrenching, all-consuming need. Their limbs entangled, and they gripped each other feverishly as they soared past time and place.

Rachel reveled in the trembling aftereffects of their passionate lovemaking as she curled up against Rafe. "It's going to work out," she whispered softly. But even as she spoke the words she wondered if she was merely trying to convince herself—or Rafe. The desperate urgency they'd both experienced left Rachel with a disturbingly anticlimactic feeling.

"We'd better get back." Rafe murmured, his voice velvety. His fingers traced her bruised lips, then he kissed her with exquisite tenderness. "It's going to work out," he confirmed huskily, then he gave her bottom a playful pinch. "Look how far we've come in such a short time."

Rachel laughed, the shadow of gloom evaporating. "We have been through a lot. It has to count for something."

"Come on," he said, tossing her suit over to her. "Besides the card from Gwen, I also received the packet from the travel agent." He gave her a teasing smile. "You still want to go through with it, don't you?"

"The wedding or the honeymoon in Paris?" she asked with mock innocence.

"Both," he said, a tantalizing smile curving his lips. "Let me warn you, before you answer, Miss Mason, that I can be a very ruthless man when thwarted."

She grinned seductively. "Oh, I know just how ruthless you can be, Kincaid. I wouldn't dream of thwarting you." She tossed her bathing suit off the blanket and provocatively edged against him. "The wedding" —she skimmed her fingertips along his inner thigh— "the honeymoon in Paris"—she pressed her lips against his earlobe—"the whole works"—she slid on top of him. "To love, honor, and cherish," she whispered, "till death do us part."

By Friday morning Rachel was feeling truly rejuvenated. Her parents had arrived from Senegal the night before; her wedding dress was ready; Monsieur Beauchamp, the caterer, had finally stopped moaning about "all of zee changes"; Norah and Josh had stopped walking around like zombies about to be cast to the wolves; and even Ned and Liz had managed another of their reconciliations. Most important of all, Rafe had been positively ebullient since their highly charged, passionate encounter on Wednesday.

Her high spirits turned out to be the calm before the storm. She sensed it the moment she walked into the breakfast room that morning and saw Norah and Josh talking in low, anxious voices with Rafe. Rafe looked up as she entered, and immediately the conversation came to an abrupt halt. Norah and Josh gave Rachel a quick glance, mumbled something in unison, and bolted out the kitchen door.

"What was that all about?" Rachel asked warily, her anxious gaze shifting from them to Rafe.

"Sit down, Rachel." He smiled, trying to counter the edge in his voice.

The smile offered no comfort. She remained standing. "What is it?"

Pain flickered in Rafe's eyes. "Rachel . . . please."

She walked on trembling legs, sinking into a seat across from him, her hands clenched together in her lap.

"I have to leave, Rachel. Right away."

Questions flashed in her mind, but she remained silent, unable to form the words.

"It's Gwen," he went on, his mouth thinned to a grim line. "She was taking some shots of a riot, and I guess the police weren't too happy with the pictures she was getting. They confiscated the camera . . . and arrested her. She was stuck in some rat-infested hole for fourteen hours before they released her." He leaned across the table. "Once she got out, she decided she really wanted out. She hopped the first plane to civilization." He hesitated. "It's my assignment, Rachel. I'm responsible. The magazine wants this thing wrapped up. I'll be back in a week . . . two at the most."

"The magazine could find a replacement for you. Was that my delusion the other day, or were you the one telling me that no one is indispensable?" Her voice sounded dry and raspy.

He looked at her for a long minute. "There's no time to dig up a substitute. They're not that easy to come by." He took in a harsh breath. "Besides, I've never skipped out on an assignment. And I'm not about to start now."

"I see." She stared at him, but her blank expression offered no clue to the churning feelings surging inside of her.

"Please try to understand, Rachel. I can't turn my back—"

She laughed harshly. "Not on your work. No, you could never turn your back on your work. But turning your back on me . . . well, that's obviously something you've already had practice doing. This time it's no doubt easier to manage." Her words were coldly etched, but her chest constricted and she felt a searing pain streak through her body. She wanted to scream, to cry, to make him see somehow that he was destroying their last chance.

"Don't talk that way, Rachel," he said sharply. "If

you can't understand, what chance do we have? Look, we can meet in Paris in two weeks, get married there, and then have our honeymoon, just like we originally planned."

Rachel said nothing.

The lines of Rafe's mouth tightened, but he gazed at her despairingly, feeling her slip away, knowing that if he left now, he could be closing the door between them forever. But he had no choice, and if Rachel couldn't see that, then he was afraid that door had already slammed shut without either of them realizing it. Rachel's words confirmed his fear.

She looked at him with icy resignation. "You never meant to give up taking overseas assignments, did you?"

Rafe paused. "I thought at first I could. But don't you see, Rachel, to give it up completely isn't the answer. That's not compromise; it's capitulation. I know in the past I used poor judgment. I ran off on every damn story that came my way. It will be different this time. But I see now that I can't make a promise I'll end up resenting having made. Please, trust me, Rachel; give us a chance."

"We don't stand a chance. I see that now. We never did." She stood up, turned away from Rafe, and started for the door.

"Don't walk out, Rachel." A pulse throbbed at his temple.

Rachel's hand reached out to the doorway to steady herself, but she didn't turn around to face him. "I'm not the one walking out, Rafe," she said in a low, resolute voice.

An hour later, bags packed, he knocked on her bedroom door. "Rachel." He tested the knob when she didn't answer; he was not surprised to find it locked.

He leaned against the door, closing his eyes tightly. "Rachel, it isn't over between us. It's never going to be over. You know that as well as I do."

He waited for some sign, anything . . . just something to cling to. But behind that locked door Rachel remained stoically silent. He glanced down at his watch. If he didn't leave now, he'd never make his plane. He tapped the packet he was holding in his hand, then bent and placed it in front of Rachel's door.

An hour later Norah found Rachel sitting off in an isolated spot at the cove.

"If you want to be left alone, just say the word," Norah said gently.

Rachel didn't answer; she didn't even acknowledge her sister's presence. Norah sat down on the sand beside her.

"I'm so sorry, Rachel."

"Does everyone know?" Her voice sounded like it came from some far-off place.

"Rafe explained. They all feel terrible, but they understand."

"Do they?" Rachel stared at the gently rolling waves.

"What will you do?" Norah asked softly.

182

"Go on . . . like none of it ever really happened," Rachel said evenly.

"He loves you, Rachel. He'll be back in a couple of weeks. Okay, so the plans for a double wedding are spoiled. But . . . that's all it means. Nothing else has to change."

"Nothing else has changed." She laughed mirthlessly. "That's the problem. It's all the same. Last time he at least managed to make it to the wedding. This time . . . well, even that proved too difficult. No, Norah. It's over." Tears spiked her eyes. She looked at her sister, feeling chilled in spite of the blazing summer sun. "We came so close. We came so damn close."

On the day of Norah's wedding Rachel managed by some miracle of inner strength to pull herself together —or at least go through the motions as if she had. She plastered a cheerful smile on her face, glad, at least, to have the condolences over with. Dressed and ready for the ceremony, she knocked on Norah's door, then opened it a crack.

"Can I help?"

"Are you kidding? Get in here before I go stark raving mad. Either Naomi was drunk when she did the final touch up on this wedding gown, or I've lost ten pounds in the last twenty-four hours."

Rachel grinned as she looked at her sister staring morosely in the mirror at the drooping gown. "You forgot the underslip, silly." She set her clutch bag on the bureau and went to the closet, pulling out the special satin liner. Norah stepped out of the gown, and Rachel helped her on with the slip and then did up the gown once again. "There." Rachel smiled. "You look beautiful, Norah. Really you do. A beautiful, radiant bride." She bit down on her lip, fighting back tears.

Norah turned to her. "Listen to me, Rachel. One last speech and then I give up. For five years now you must have met a dozen or more perfectly respectable, nice men . . . men who could offer you all the stability and security your little heart could desire. Now, why do you suppose you've never been tempted by a single one of them? I'll tell you why."

Rachel had to laugh. "I'm sure you will."

"Because, for all his reckless, erratic, impossible behavior, you happen to be in love with Rafe Kincaid. Maybe he won't change, Rachel. Maybe he can't give you a traditional, safe, secure life. But don't you realize he gives you something else that's more important? He makes you feel alive, Rachel. He breathes fire and spirit into you. And you do the same for him."

Rachel touched Norah's cheek. Then she opened her purse to take out a small gold locket for her sister to wear. "Something borrowed," she said softly, placing it carefully around her sister's neck. She gave her a tender hug. "I wish you all of the happiness in the world, Norah."

Norah hugged her back. "I want you to be happy, too, Rachel. Will you . . . think about what I said?"

Rachel's eyes drifted to her open purse on the bureau. She could make out the blue edge of the thin packet Rafe had left for her. Inside was one plane ticket for Paris, a simple gold wedding band, and the hotel reservation for the honeymoon suite whose windows overlooked the Seine. And a note that simply said, *"Toujours amour."*

Rachel smiled hesitantly. "I will think about it."

By Monday morning, the festivities over, Rachel gave up thinking. She felt alone, empty. Yesterday afternoon she'd watched her sister and Josh join hands in holy matrimony. Witnessing their joy, she'd felt an excruciating ache inside of her. She missed Rafe desperately. Sorting it out suddenly felt pointless. When had being rational and reasonable ever worked where she and Rafe were concerned? Their love was impulsive, volatile, impossible, but vital to them both. Even a hurricane couldn't stop it. She remembered Rafe's words in that dark cellar beneath the boat house during the storm. He told her that she was his roots. And finally Rachel saw that it was equally true for her. He was her love, her second heartbeat, the source of her joy and happiness.

Five hours later she was on a plane for Paris, gold band in her purse, wedding gown neatly packed in her suitcase. She had no idea if Rafe would really show. He'd told her two weeks at the most.

A faint smile curved her lips. He'd asked her to trust him. Well, she was finally ready. She might not know exactly when he'd get to Paris, but she knew that she would be there waiting for him.

* * *

In a dank, squalid hut in the hills of Managua, Rafe lay on a straw mat tossing a small gold object absently in the air. He was drenched in sweat, and although it was two in the morning, he found it impossible to sleep. His inability to drift off had nothing to do with the heat, the insects swarming around the room, or even the fact that his last day's shooting had gone even lousier than those of the previous five days. It was Rachel who kept him awake. Images of Rachel absorbed him, making mincemeat of his previously cool, analytical, photojournalistic vision. He'd snap a shot and there she'd be, clouding his view of the scene. He couldn't get her out of his mind. She clung to him like a second skin. She was a part of him, the part that made everything else worthwhile. With sudden clarity Rafe Kincaid finally saw what he'd always fought so hard to accept. He needed her. He needed Rachel to make life complete.

He stopped tossing the gold object and studied it in the palm of his hand. It was a wedding band, one that matched the ring he'd left for Rachel. His eyes glistened as he stared at it.

He got up from the hard straw mat and glanced at his camera, lying on a low wooden table. He had more than a week before the final deadline, plenty of time to make up for what were probably the crummiest shots he'd ever taken in his life.

He shrugged, a small smile curving his lips. On the other hand, if he left now, he'd get to Paris much

186

sooner than he'd promised Rachel. He could be there waiting for her. The fleeting thought that she might not show at all crossed his mind, but he just as quickly dismissed it. She had to show. He pressed his lips to the gold band, then tucked it safely in his pocket. He'd have to dig up a good Parisian photographer to snap their wedding picture.

She was fast asleep, a warm night breeze drifting off the Seine through the French windows. She rolled onto her side, one hand curled over her head, the other pressed between her naked thighs.

She was having a delightful dream, and when the bed sagged at one end and a warm male body pressed up against her, it fit quite splendidly into the scene. She sighed lustily as a strong, knowing hand slipped up her rib cage and cupped her breast.

It was only when a low, seductive voice whispered her name that she realized it was no dream. Her eyes shot open.

"Rafe?" Her voice trembled as warm lips traveled down her back.

"Expecting someone else?"

She laughed softly, happily, as she rolled over to face him. Then she slid into his arms, relishing the feel of his strong, familiar body. She pressed her lips to his. "No. No, my darling. Only you. Always you."